Leon left school at the beginning of the eighties with little to no education; he came to understand later in life that he suffers from dyslexia. If it had not been for laptops and spell check, this novel may never have happened. Leon lives in Suffolk, UK, and is single.

George Alfred Watkins and Florence Cristabel Tricker—two of the most wonderful and inspiring souls.

Leon Gordon Moak McAvoy

A BOY FROM THE VALLEYS

AUSTIN MACAULEY PUBLISHERS™

LONDON • CAMBRIDGE • NEW YORK • SHARJAH

A CIP catalogue record for this title is available from the British Library.

ISBN 9781528918190 (Paperback)
ISBN 9781528918206 (Hardback)
ISBN 9781528962223 (Epub e-book)

www.austinmacauley.com

First Published (2020)
Austin Macauley Publishers Ltd
25 Canada Square
Canary Wharf
London
E14 5LQ

To my mother, Gloria Jean Watkins-McAvoy, for your support and encouragement in the telling of this story.

It is said that, for a man to know where he is going in life,
He must first know from where he came.

My name is George Alfred Watkins,
A boy from the Valleys
And this is my story.

George Watkins Senior was born in 1859 to parents, Joseph and Mary, in Kington, Herefordshire. He had ten brothers and sisters, Margaret, Thomas, Ann, Ruth, Wells, Jane, Maryann, Jane, Joseph and Michael. Of the eleven children, there were three sets of twins, George being one set with his twin sister, Jane. Their father, Joseph, was a miner who worked underground and had little to no education.

George Senior himself was a miner who also worked underground. In 1884, he met his wife, Dinah Simmonds, from Mountain Ash Glamorgan, Wales, and they married when Dinah was eighteen. They lived at 4 Dover Street Mountain Ash, a two up two down Victorian terrace, the front door went directly onto a cobbled street, a small back-garden with an outhouse toilet, coal shed, and over thirteen years, had eight children, Thomas, David, Amelia, Alice, Emily, George H, Sarah A, and George Alfred; Amelia and Alice were twins.

In 1896, when Dinah Watkins had her seventh child, Sarah Annie, they were still living in Mountain Ash close to the railway line.

In early 1896, George and Dinah were visited by his brother, Joseph, five years his senior. Joseph then lived in Wales but some distance away from Mountain Ash and had a wife, Mary, and four children. Joseph casually worked as a labourer.

It was early evening, George Senior swinging his lunch pail walked home after a long hard day underground at the colliery, pulling the black gold from the ground. The men were covered in coal dust from head to toe, their clothes were caked thick with the stuff, only the whites of their eyes and the occasional smile of white teeth gave away features of their faces. Dinah had boiled a large pan of water on the coal-fired stove and prepared a small tin bath in the backyard where George was now washing the coal soot from his body. This was a common practice of the day, a way in which the lady of the house could only but try and keep this black dust, which coated the entire village from entering the house. You could say the residue from this black gold was in their blood but it was also visible in a person spit whenever they spat.

There came a knock at the door which was completely unexpected at this time of the day, a time when the evening meal was being prepared.

Dinah looked up from the stove and said, "Who on earth can this be? I'm about to dish up." On opening the door, there stood Joseph, George's older brother, dressed in a large over-coat, flat cap and boots to guard against the cold. In one hand, he was holding a stone demijohn and had obviously come directly from the inn.

Doffing his cap, Joseph said, "Hello, Dinah, and how is my favourite sister-in-law on this fine Glamorgan evening?" Looking over his shoulder, Dinah could see the usual persistent drizzle was still coming down.

Dinah opened the door with the words, "You can leave those muddy boots out there." Joseph complied with a grin, more from the alcohol he had consumed then meeting his sister-in-law.

Dinah was unsure of Joseph, it wasn't something she could put her finger on, it was more down to a women's intuition.

George came in from the backyard half-dressed rubbing his hair with a towel. "Was that the door I could hear, Dinah? Oh, hello, Joseph, what brings you here?"

"Don't ask, George," said Joseph.

Dinah said, "I gather you'll be stopping for supper."

"That would be very kind of you, Dinah," said Joseph. As all good mothers, they somehow managed to make rations stretch to feed another mouth.

"How is Mary and the children?" said Dinah.

"More trouble than there's worth," said Joseph, turning to George and holding up the demijohn. "Come, brother, have a drink with me."

"I'll have a small cup, Joseph, but I must to be up early for work tomorrow so I'll have to take it easy." George wasn't so much intimidated by Joseph, but he was his older brother and thus commanded respect.

The two men sat, George pulling on a clean shirt as Dinah placed two cups on the table and poured both men a shot of whisky. "Children, supper is ready," Dinah called and from all corners of the house came a riotous clatter of excited children. They became wearily as they entered the room to find Joseph.

"Your uncle Joseph is eating with us tonight, say hello," said Dinah. Some did and some just mouthed the words. Amelia, one of the twins, slid onto George's lap and stared at Joseph.

After a hearty supper and a couple more cups of whisky for the men, Dinah ordered the children upstairs whilst she cleared the table. On turning with dishes, Joseph reached out and tapped Dinah on the behind, all the time staring at George. "You have a good one here, George," he said. It was an awkward moment that neither George nor Dinah knew how to react to.

After the dishes were cleared, Dinah announced she would put the children to bed and retire herself. "Nice to see you again, Joseph," she said and left the room.

The two men sat by the fire light sipping whisky and recalling life, growing up in a large family.

George woke early, it was still dark, quietly, he rolled from bed and reached for where he had left the clothes the night before. Stumbling, he remembered he had also been a drinking. Dinah wouldn't rise with him at this time, it was too early to rouse the children, even on a school day. George gathered his lunch pail that Dinah had prepared the night before and all that he needed for another long day at the face.

By the time George strode into work, it was becoming light, still raining but not so hard for mid-February, all in all, he felt OK.

The colliery in Cynon Valley of 1896 didn't employ many men, surprisingly, and considering it supplied a large proportion of the world's coal due to the fact that the coal burnt cleanly. It was a busy mine, a mine that was one of the deepest mines in the region.

As George walked up to the lifts at the shaft entrance, he was met by the pit manager, Mr Henry. "Morning, George," he said. "Looks like spring is on its way."

"Morning, boss, it certainly does," replied George. All the men working there were on good friendly terms as most mining communities were, you never knew when tragedy would strike as it had on many occasions, just recently, due to men smoking below ground and igniting gases.

George entered the cage with a dozen or so other men to a chorus of good morning and began the slow descent of a thousand feet or more.

As George descended into the darkness, there came a feeling of unwell, not a hangover, he had learnt over many years to deal with those. No, there was something else he couldn't quite put his finger on, something just didn't sit right at the back of his mind. From darkness came the dim glimmer of lantern light as the cage came to a stop and the men filed out into the usual oppressive low ceilings that now rapped themselves around them.

George walked crouched back to the seam where he had been working the day before, hung his jacket, grab his pike and began the hard, heavy hot work of extracting the black gold.

From out of the dark came echoes of conversation the night before. "Don't ask," was the reply from Joseph when asked about his family at home. Why was he here? Why travel so far just to see them? He had laid a hand upon his wife, brother or not, this wasn't acceptable behaviour. Why had he not said something there and then? "You've a good one there, George." *But he had been drinking, he was just being family, wasn't he? I'm being silly,* George said to himself.

But no matter how hard he tried, he could not shake off these thoughts, and with a sharp stab to the stomach like a knife, he turned and said to his friend beside him, "Something wrong." George dropped his pick, turned on his heels and half-ran back down the shaft to the lift cage. "Take me to the top, John," he said the lift master.

"What's wrong, George? Are you unwell?"

"Just get me up as quick as you can, John."

"OK, but I'll have inform Mr Henry, we're a man down, George."

"Yes, yes I'll make good later," said George.

The temperature at the surface most certainly wasn't cold but the difference from that and underground temperature was definitely noticeably. In his rush, he had left his jacket behind.

George ran, he knew not why, he dare not begin to believe his fears. *It's Joseph, he's my brother, he would not surely.* But he knew something was wrong. At each turn, his hobnail boots slid on wet cobble, he barely kept his balance at times.

At the house, Dinah had risen, got the children washed and fed, and for those old enough and lucky enough to have a place, off to school they went in good time. Slumped in the arm chair by the fire, Joseph still sat half-awake, he had consumed much more liquor than George the night before, not including what he had drunk at the inn before he was asked to leave by the inn keeper.

"I have some hot tea, Joseph, if you'd like some," said Dinah.

"Where does George keep the whiskey?" he said. There was whisky in the house, but Dinah wasn't letting on as to where it was, Joseph was still clearly under the influence. Joseph rose up from the chair too unsteady for a man his size. "This is not the hospitality I expect from my brother's house nor his wife," he said in a raised voice. "Dinah, fetch the whiskey I said."

Startled, Dinah said, "Please, Joseph, have some hot tea and I'll make you some food, it will make you feel better."

Joseph crossed the kitchen in two strides, and with the back of his large hand, struck Dinah in the face. On reeling back, she caught glimpse of the children standing at the door. "Go to the back of the house, children," she cried. Joseph stepped forward slowly undoing his belt. "Please don't beat me, Joseph," she cried.

"Oh, I'm not going to hurt you, Dinah." The realisation of what was about to occur hit her as if he had struck her again.

"No, no, please, Joseph, please, no." Joseph spun Dinah around, grabbed her by the back of her neck and push her face down onto the table, and at the same time, lifted her petticoat and skirt. All the time, Dinah kept saying, "No, Joseph, no," with sobbed pleas.

When Joseph had finished, he stood. Dinah rolled from the table, landing back against the door as if shielding the children on the other side. Joseph's face turned to the ceiling with a broad grin and he began fastening his belt and trousers as he said, "Now get me that whiskey."

The room went still, boom went the door and there stood George. His attention immediately went to Dinah, still sat on the floor, head tilted down. George rushed to her side and gently raised her face to the light. She was bleeding from her nose and a cut to her lip, barely audible, she said, "Sorry, George." The hand George was steadying himself on the floor by slowly turned to a fist, and with a roar that felt as though it came from the pits of hell itself, he sprang to his feet, launching a flurry of punches at his brother, the speed and ferocity meant that most of the blows landed on Joseph's chest. As he reeled, George slowed his pace and contact to Joseph's face was now accurate. This sent a clear signal that George's intention was to do real harm. The thwack of fist on face became sickening, and all Joseph could do was to try to make for the door, defence out of the question. Joseph fell into the street face down and on turning onto his back, he faced the sky just as the studs of a hobnail boot came crashing down.

"Never darken my door again, Joseph Watkins, you are no brother of mine." George turned and went back into the house to tend to his wife, Dinah.

It's a Boy

January 9th, 1897

Snow was falling thick and fast over the small community of Mountain Ash, and although it wasn't late in the day, lanterns were needed, particularly in the Watkins household. Dinah had gone into labour, the doctor had been called and was with her in the bedroom. George was sat downstairs by the fireplace, head in hand, he had not wanted to be at the birth. There was now silence all bare the crackly of the fire. The door latch popping up startled George and there stood the doctor, wiping his hands on a towel. "How is she?" George said, standing.

"She's tired but just fine, George." There was a pause, and with a quizzical look, the doctor said, "And you have a healthy son, George." George did not respond to this but thanked the doctor, side stepped him and went upstairs.

George entered the bedroom to find Dinah laid in bed, staring adoringly at the tiny infant in her arms. "Look, George, it's a boy," said Dinah.

George went to the bed side and held Dinah's hand, she, although tired, looked radiant and beautiful, George kissed the back of her hand, and said, "I love you," but he barely acknowledged the infant. "I'll make some tea," said George and went downstairs.

In the coming weeks and months, it was all Dinah could do to try and forge some interest from George in the child, she even named him George Alfred Watkins after George himself, but to no avail, the relationship was indifferent and George would only hold the child if he really had to.

As years went by, Dinah could only recall one conversation she and George had that directly involved George Alfred. George standing in front of the window pipe in his mouth, said, "Dinah, from now on, should anyone inquire after George Alfred, he is Sarah Annie's twin brother and was born in the same year."

This, as time went on, was not completely unfeasible due to the very small stature of both Sarah and George Alfred.

George's early years were no different from those of his brothers and sisters, and for that matter, any other child at that time. He had a loving mother in Dinah, and his brothers and sisters were doting and caring of the two youngest in the family, Sarah and George.

The relationship between George and Sarah was particularly close, growing up believing they were twins, they were inseparable, hand in hand everywhere they went. Sarah always just that little bit taller and just that little more mature, but then, everyone would say, "Oh, one twin is always the bigger, isn't it?"

"George will come good in his own time, you'll see."

George was never neglected nor left out, it wasn't that he got any less attention from his father than anyone else, who had limited amounts of time and energy to spend with any of the children due to working long hours. George Alfred, and his brothers and sisters would all celebrate birthdays and Christmas, and would all get presents. George and Sarah were particularly blessed at birthdays as they celebrated theirs together so double the fun and excitement.

There was ample food and George always had clothes on his back albeit hand-me-downs which would tend to drown him until his mother, Dinah, weaved her magic with needle and thread, and he looked quite passable.

The community was always good like that as there was always someone's son or daughter just growing out of clothes and boots, however, George would always seem more at home barefoot in the summer months.

By the time George was five, he knew the surrounding hills, valleys, streams and fields but always stayed far away from the railroad tracks as Dinah told him. It would seem everyone knew little George, the practical joker, but to his credit, a polite, courteous and friendly child, he was never ever naughty and never complained, and would always be seen with a smile on his cheeky little face, Dinah adored him.

August 11th, 1903, Mountain Ash, Glamorgan

It was warm, warm for the valleys and George found himself playing in his favourite stream, and playing his favourite game, that of George Alfred Watkins, master boat-builder.

He had never seen a boat in really life, only pictures in books, but he would wait patiently at the local green grossers for a wooden crate to become empty and the green grocer would hand them over to him with a big smile saying, "That boat of yours must be mighty big by now, George." He would carefully dismantle the box and with some twine fashion the boards into boats of various shape, and with varying success as far as floatability was concerned. His sister wasn't with him on this day, his sisters and some of his brothers had been given more chores around the house recently due to his mother, Dinah, not being well of late.

He didn't mind being on his own. His sister, Sarah Annie, didn't so much like boats but did like wading in water up to her knees and watching tiddlers dart in and out of her legs.

George had just launched his latest creation from the other side of the bridge, he would run alongside guiding the boat with the longest stick he was able to hold, the sun was glistening on the water which made it hard at times to see the silhouette of the boat. He would often wonder where the stream went and what adventures would lay beyond. George did indeed wish to build a boat that would, one day, carry him, perhaps to those adventures.

Just then, George thought he heard his name being called, but it couldn't be time for supper. He looked up at the sun, it was too high, too early for supper, and went about chasing the boat again. Over the hill came his old brother, David, and he called his name. David was fifteen, and by all accounts, a man. He had gone to work with their father at the pit.

"George, come away now, you're needed at home."

"But why?" he said. "It's not supper time."

"Do as you're told, come now." George looked back to see his boat rounding the bend and disappearing out of sight on to adventures he could all but dream of.

"Am I in trouble?" George said, trying to keep pace with David.

"No," said David.

"Then what?" said George, but David said no more.

As they turned into Dover street, George could see some of the neighbours stood outside of his house holding their children by the hand. As he and his brother approached, they looked at George with frowns on their faces. Whatever it was he'd done, it must be serious.

George was rushed into the house and up the stairs. Why were all his brothers and sisters not in school, and why was David not at work and why was his father here during day light? George was pushed into the bedroom in front of his brother, David. This made him feel a little uncomfortable as he nor any of his brothers and sisters were allowed into their mother and father's room unless they were sent to fetch an article of clothing or a brush. Other than that, it was generally out of bounds.

There laid on the bed was his mother, Dinah, propped up by pillows and in her night-gown. George knew something was wrong. "There's my beautiful boy, come to me, George," Dinah said in a croaky voice. George approached the bed, and as he drew near, Dinah reached out and pulled him onto the bed with strength he wasn't expecting. Now laying fully clothed beside his mother, George was finding it very difficult to understand what was happening. Then Dinah, with her arms wrapped around him, kissed the top of his head, she then tilted his head back and looked directly into his eyes as hers teared up. "George, my beautiful little George, you be a good boy for your father now, do you hear?"

"Yes, Mother," said George, one of Dinah's tear now falling to his check.

"I love you so much, my little man, now go downstairs with your sister, Sarah, and your brother, George. Sally from next-door will take care of you for now."

George, and his brother and sister were whisked out of the darkened room and down the stairs, and out into a contrastingly bright summer's day.

George became lost in playing with the neighbours' children, but sometime later, his older brothers and sisters came filing out of the house one by one, heads in hands and sobbing. George kept asking what had happened but no one spoke, he would not see his father for the rest of that day.

Dinah died that afternoon of heart disease, she was 37.

George's grandmother, Sarah, arrived that same afternoon and immediately took charge. Sarah was a practical women, used to organising a large family. She was beautiful, long dark hair, although she was starting to go grey. It was clear where Dinah had got her looks. She, Sarah, set about busying the older children with chores and tasks in order to keep them occupied, and the three youngest were allowed to play with the next-door children whilst food was prepared and dinner served at the same time. Nothing seemed to change that much except for peoples demeanour. George knew then that he had lost his mother.

Over the next three days, George and his sister, Sarah, spent most of their time in the company of their grandmother, going from one official-looking building to the next. Sarah signed her daughter's death certificate with her moniker as she could not read nor write. This was usually done by the surviving husband or wife but George Senior was in no fit state at this time, he was having trouble coming to terms with the loss of his beloved wife so young.

The following day, his grandmother took himself and his sister, Sarah, to the local seamstress in the village. She was a large lady who greeted them as if they had been friends for years. George didn't mind, hers was the first smiling face he'd seen in the last two days. The seamstress would buy clothing that people couldn't pass down and refurb those to resale. His sister, Sarah, came away with a new summer frock. George fared much better, coming away with a new jacket, trousers and a shirt. He felt torn between great sadness and a certain amount of joy on receiving a whole new set of cloths.

On the way back home, they stopped at the tailors in the high street and there George was presented with a shelf full of brand-new flat caps and was told he could choose one. He could not believe his good fortune, this had never happened to him before, and so he took his time placing three or four on his head and looking at himself in the mirror before he chose a plain black one. The tailor confirming he had indeed made, "An excellent choice, sir." The cap was wrapped in brown paper and handed to him as his grandmother paid.

George couldn't thank his grandmother enough for all the gifts but his gratefulness seemed to be met with some indifference.

On arriving home, George wanted to share his excitement with everyone about his new clothes but was told to hush, for there in the front room propped up on two wooden trestles was a black coffin, its lid on but, by the way, people would stop and pause by it told George his mother lay within.

Once the family had eaten and the dishes were cleared away, the younger children were washed and put to bed. Again, their father had not joined them. There was a certain amount of coming and going that night, voices long into the early hours. George didn't sleep, for every time he closed his eyes, he could see flashers of light and images of his mother, and he had heard his name mentioned downstairs on many occasion. Or was it someone referring to his father? It was a relief when dawn came.

He Has to Go

Dawn saw the whole family up. His grandmother preparing breakfast, sisters and brothers helping each other to wash, dress and do hair. George's new clothes had been laid out, and there at the bottom of his bed were his boots gleaming from being diligently polished with great care.

George, now dressed and looking very smart, if he said so himself, stood in front of the mirror with his brand new cap. First, he worn it to the left at a slight jaunty angle and then to the right same angle, and then turned it around and wore it backwards and instantly decided that looked silly, and as he moved to place it properly, his grandmother appeared, lifted the cap and plonked it back down on his head the right way around saying, "This way, George." He knew and he felt stupid that his grandmother had caught him fooling around.

There came the sound of cart wheels on cobbles stone from the street, and the household as one rose and filed outside without a word, except for his brothers, Thomas, David, his father and grandfather, Thomas, who had arrived at the family home the night before.

The four men came out of the house carrying Dinah's coffin and placed it onto the bed of the cart, the family lined up behind. The man prompted the horse and the cart, and family moved off, followed closely by a crowd of friends and neighbours.

The cemetery was only a short journey away. On coming to a halt, the four men lifted Dinah from the bed of the cart and walked coffin on shoulders, a short walk to a freshly dug grave, the soil piled to one side, so fresh, in fact, George could see worms within it and couldn't help thinking how good they would be for fishing down at the stream.

A man of religion stood at the head of the grave and proceeded to say things George couldn't understand. George looked at his father, he hadn't seen for the last few days. George had always seen his father as quite a young man but now he looked older, gaunt pale, black beneath his eyes, eyes wide non-blinking, staring at something on the ground some six feet ahead, but George couldn't see anything on the ground that his father was looking at. The ceremony came to an end and the same four men lowered Dinah into the ground and the assembled crowd slowly moved away.

The following day, people were busy, preparations being made so much so, George manage to slip away to the stream. He didn't have with him any materials for making boats and didn't want to, he was just content to sit on the bank and watch the water slide by. She had looked so well laid in her coffin as if nothing was ailing her, as if she was just asleep, he missed his mother and he knew he always would, George for the first time in private sobbed.

George stayed there for as long as he could, until he knew he had to go home as it was close to supper time. He turned into the street and it was the same old street, children playing, dogs barking, nothing had changed in this world as it had in his.

That night, George did manage to get some sleep but it was more to do with emotional fatigue than natural tiredness. He was woken by his grandmother early, and told to rise and wash as she had breakfast ready. There at the foot of his bed were his new clothes and boots. George washed, got dressed, and ate a breakfast of bread and pork fat. He ate alone, his grandmother flittering about in the kitchen. He guessed his bothers were at work, sisters at school and his closest sister, Sarah, was still in bed, tired from the day before. As George finished his mug of sweet tea, his father appeared, he sat at the table and drank a cup of tea. George Alfred not saying anything, not knowing what to say.

George Senior rose, pulled out his pocket watch and said to Sarah, his mother-in-law, "We must be off." Sarah came to his side and placed a reassuring hand on his shoulder. "Come on, George," said his father, the statement startled him.

"Go? Go where, Father?" George's grandmother, without word, came over and kissed George on the head, and then placed his cap straight and correct. On stepping into the street, his father took him by the hand, the other hand holding a long canvas bag that had a strap attached for carrying. They walked to the end of the street. George naturally wanting to step to the right, they turned left, a direction George never went because he had been told by his mother never to as this direction led to the railway line.

George and his father walked onto the platform, and there stood a steam train, a huge iron machine hissing and bellowing smoke. George's father had words with the conductor, and turned to George and knelt before him. He pulled two pieces of paper from his pocket, one, he poked into the breast pocket of George's jacket, the other, a liable with string attached which he tied through the hole in the lapel of his jacket. "George," his father said whilst holding him by his arms, "I have to send you away."

"Where?" said George.

"Not far," said his father.

"But why?" said George.

"Since your mother passed away, George, I have found that I can't take care of you. So I'm sending you to somewhere they can."

"But why?" said George, panic in his voice. "I'll be good, Father. I promise, Father." His father looked at the ground. "I promised Mother I'd be good and I won't eat much, I promise."

His father took the bag from his shoulder and placed it onto George's, and said, "Don't make a fuss, George," and turned the boy around and lifted him onto the top step of the carriage. He followed George into the first compartment and sat him down against the window. Kneeling down, he took George's cap off and placed it on his lap, and holding his hand, simply said, "Be the best man you can, George," stood up, turned and left.

George Senior stepped back onto the platform and walked to the exit. As he came to the end of the railings, he stopped, grief hitting him hard, so hard, he had to reach out and grab the railings to steady himself. He looked to the floor, and under his breath, he said, "Oh, Dinah, what have I done." He straightened himself, let go of the railings and quickly turned the corner.

George was the only person in the carriage, he was frozen with fear, he dare not move nor breathe, he was then gripped with the urge to turn and look in the direction his father had gone. He had to overcome his fear, he had to force himself to turn and now.

He spun in his seat and peered down the platform, just in time to see his father disappearing around the corner at the end of the railings and he was gone.

The sharp shrill of a whistle startled him and he sat back in his seat. The sound of the large engine roared into life and the train jerked. The couplings clanking and all went quite again. *Were we moving?* George thought. He couldn't tell, he stared at the station sign to get some sort of barring, the sign said 'Mountain Ash' and yes, very, very slowly, the train began to roll. As the sign glided out of sight, it would be the very last time he would see Mountain Ash and the very last time he would see or hear anything of his family ever again. George was now on his own.

The door at the end of the carriage opened and the conductor came in. He wore a jacket, waist coat with a chain and watch, trousers of the same colour and a cap that stood up on his head with some kind of railway symbol on the front. He had large whiskers down each side of his large red face, he walked to the boy with a pair of silver clippers in his hand and took the ticket from George's breast pocket, held it up inspected it, clipped a hole in one corner and placed it back into his pocket. He then picked up the label, still attached to George's lapel with string and read what was on it and then placed it back. The conductor looked at George and said, "You're getting off at Cardiff, it's the end of the line." Sensing that George had no idea what he had just said, the conductor, with a hint of kindness on his face, said, "Don't worry, I'll come and get you when we're there," and then walked on to the next carriage.

George looked down at the label, picking it up, he looked at what was written on it. It meant nothing to him as George couldn't read, but if he had, he would have read, *George Alfred Watkins 6, Care of 15, Moira Terrace, Cardiff.*

The train picked up pace and George found that there was a rhythm and rhyme to the sound which was almost hypnotic and he began to repeat it in his mind, *da da, d dum da da, d dum da da, d dum*. This, coupled with the gentle swaying from side to side, the motion reminded George of when he would sit on his mother's knee, and she would wrap her arms around him and sway to and throw, singing gently in his ear, his heart sank to the pit of his stomach and he turned his attention to the outside world.

A world he could just about recognise, for there were the hills and valleys and streams, but he had never seen them pass by at such speed. He was mesmerised, he tried to focus on sheep in fields but found his eyes couldn't fix nor focus correctly, it was blurring his vision. All the time, the 'da da, d dum' seemed to just get quicker and quicker, surely not, surely, this machine he was in couldn't get any faster. George thought that if he had been outside, traveling at this speed, he would almost certainly suffocate. Just then, the rhythm slowed and into view came a station. Just for a moment, George thought he was back at Mountain Ash, the station looking almost identical but he knew it wasn't and his heart sank once more.

The train slowed gently and then came to a sudden halt which threw George forward on his shiny leather seat and it unnerved him. Just when he thought he had got the measure of this beast, it surprised him yet again, what more does it have in store for him. There was a hustle and bustle on the platform, and George could hear doors opening and closing and he found himself saying, "Please don't come into this carriage, please." George just wanted to be on his own, the door clicked and swung open, and in came a small girl. She was wearing pantaloons that met her tall boots at her shins, a blouse and a wide brim straw hat. Her mother walked in behind her, she was wearing a long skirt, blouse and, again, a wide brim hat but this was of a fabric material, and behind her, a tall man in a tailored-suit and boots of a fancy nature, the like of which George had never seen before. As he stepped in, he removed the high-bowler hat. The girl went to sit opposite George but was shooed away by her mother, and the family then sat and settled on the other side of the carriage.

The high shrill of the whistle broke the air and George jumped out of his skin, and immediately, felt silly that he had been caught out once again. The train moved out and soon came the reassuring 'da da, d dum'.

George once again watched as the world whizzed by and got the feeling he was being watched, and from the corner of his eye, saw that the girl was now staring directly at him. He turned and their eyes meet, she smiled and George, sensing a friend within her, smiled back. The girl's mother nudged her and frowned disapprovingly. The lady looked over George slowly, from boots to head, and George got the feeling that she was judging him and not kindly.

George settled in and looked out of the window taking breaks periodically as it made him dizzy. *Where ever it was that the beast was taking me, it must be a long, long way away,* he thought, so it came as a surprise that mountain, valley and field began to give way to houses, factories and important-looking buildings and people, lots and lots of people, more people he had seen in one place ever.

The family opposite suddenly rose and began readying themselves. The tempo of the train began to slow, and once again, a station came into view. George knew what was coming and readied himself for the halt. He successfully kept himself in place by holding on to the seat, feeling quite proud of himself for doing so, looked to the family for approval but they had already left the carriage and were stepping onto the platform. As they went past the window, the little girl, now holding her mother's hand, looked back at George and they smiled, and George felt some comfort.

Cardiff City, Wales

The engine died and a cacophony of noise took over, the sound of people going about their hurried business. George sat and wondered what to do. Just then, the conductor appeared and said, "We here, boy. Cardiff, come with me." George gathered his bag, slid off the seat and followed. Unable to climb down the steep steps of the train, George jumped, he had arrived. The conductor walked George a short distance to the station office, turned and said, "Stand here, boy, and someone will collect you." George said, "Thank you," but the conductor had already disappeared into the crowd.

Watching a sea of people going to and throw in front of him so deep, he couldn't see through them. George became so wrapped up with this scene that he was startled when a large hand came from nowhere and grabbed at the label on his lapel. George looked up to see a portly gentleman, dishevelled hair, round red face, working jacket and trousers but what caught George's eye was the thick black belt with large brass buckle that seemed to hold this man together at the middle. Having studied the label, the man leaned in and said, "Right, come with me, boy," turned and stepped away.

George found it difficult to keep pace. *Why was everything so fast here?*

On leaving the station, George was ill-prepared for the scene that greeted him. He was used to by now, the amount of people, but the buildings were so high and horses, and a street so wide, it would take him minutes to cross if it wasn't for the carts and there, for the first time, George saw a cart with no horse. It was a machine, not like the train, no, smaller, and it had people in, but no horses. George was rooted to the spot in ore. "Oh," came the voice of the man who had collected him. "I haven't got all day." He stood by a buggy with one horse to the front, he guested to the back and George climbed aboard. As they trotted on, George peered over the side of the buggy as they clopped along, and the scene went on and on.

They turned into Moira Terrace and came to a holt. The man clamber down and directed George to the front door of a terrace house, three storeys high. At the door stood a woman dressed in a black dress with a white pinafore tied at the back, she wore a white bonnet covering black and grey hair. "Is this him?" she said.

"It is," said the man.

"I'm Mistress Evans and I run this house. This is the one and only time you will enter this house by the front door, you come and go by the back entrance from now on. Do you hear?" George nodded. The woman took George by the hand and they walked into the hallway. The floors were wooden and polished, there were rugs on the floor which George tripped over. As they passed a door on the right, George could see a grand fireplace and large leather furniture and mirrors, and a chandelier. Mistress Evans stopped George and said, "You are not allowed in this part of the house, do you hear?" Again, George nodded.

At the end of the corridor, they came to a door that led down into the basement where the kitchen was located. A large wooden table took pride of place in the centre of the room. "This is where you'll eat," she said. Just then, from a side door that led to a courtyard, a boy came sliding to an abrupt stop and stared at Mistress Evans as though he had just been caught doing something naughty. "Ah, Thomas, take this lad and show him his bed."

"Yes, Mistress," said Thomas.

Thomas was about two years older than George, dressed in clothes that had seen better days, he was thin and pale. Thomas waited until they were out of ear shot of Mistress Evans as they walked upstairs and said, "What's your name?"

"I'm George Alfred Watkins," said George.

"I asked for your name, not your title," said Thomas. They climbed another set of stairs and walked through one of two doors off that landing. The room had bear floorboards, there was a dormer window at each end, one looked into the Moira Terrace and the other, the courtyard at the rear. Thomas pointed to the bed opposite the door and said, "This used to be my bed, it's your turn now." George didn't understand what Thomas meant but didn't question.

Thomas left George to unpack his bag into the small locker beside the bed, and sat down and waited.

George had sat there so long, he began to think they had forgotten about him. He listened to the noise outside of people going to and throw. Occasionally, he would get up and go to the window to look out, only to rush back to the bed when he heard a noise downstairs. It was on one of these visits to the window that George spotted the man who had picked him up from the station, lumbering along at the head of a procession of girls. The first, about his chest height, then going down in size to the last not much smaller than George. All in line and holding hands as they went. The girls were dressed in grey dresses and bib, black stockings and ankle boots, with a grey bonnet on their heads, hair tucked in. They disappeared from view just as a cart rounded the corner at the end of the street. The man sat upfront holding the reins was dressed very shabbily, the horse drawing the cart looked tired and had seen better days. The cart pulled to a holt directly outside of the house, and as the man dismounted, so did three boys from the back of the cart and scattered instantly.

George heard the front door deep down in the front of the house slam, and there appeared a man trotting down the steps and into the street. The two men approached, there was no handshake but it was obvious they were acquainted.

The man who had left the house was dressed all in black, black pointed shoe, tight trousers, a long coat and vest with pocket watch and chain. The only article of clothing not black was a white shirt, the collar and cuffs standing out against the black. At his neck, a cravat, and on his head, a short top-hat which he wore at a slight angle, whiskers of hair protruding from beneath. Because of the hat, George could not quite see his face but didn't try too hard to do so, for George was drawn to what the man was holding in his hand, a black shiny cane with a silver tip and rounded head. The man wheeled this cane provocatively as an extension of himself. The two men greeted and began to engage. George couldn't hear what their conversation was but the rough-looking man, who had climbed down from the cart, was clearly not happy about something and the man in black was clearly trying to appease him jesting back towards the house with the cane. The two men paused and the rough-looking man not breaking his stare from the man in black, dipped his fingers into waistcoat pocket, and produced something and handed it to him. The man in black tipped his hat barely, turned and hopped back up the house stairs, and again, the door deep down below slammed closed. At this, George shot back to his bed and sat.

As soon as George could hear no one was coming for him just yet, he jumped up and went to the rear window, the one looking down over the yard. Here were assemble the boys and girls, some washing from pails, some removing clothes and handing them to Mistress Evans who was barking orders, chasing and herding them as if they were wild chickens.

Just then, there was a sound from the stairs and George was back at his bed before the door was slung open. It was Thomas and George let go of the breath he was holding. "They're back," said Thomas.

"Do they all live here too?" said George.

"Yes," said Thomas. "The girls in the room next door and the boys sleep in here with us."

"Where have they been?" said George.

"To work," said Thomas. "Have you unpacked?"

"Yes," said George.

"Good, it's supper time," said Thomas. "And by the way, you'll be coming to work with me on Monday."

"Work?" said George.

"Yes, everyone has to earn their keep here, George. You're going to work for 'The muck man'," said Thomas with a smile that made George feel uneasy. Thomas removed George's cap and went to throw it onto the pillow of George's bed, stopped and looked at it, and said, "This is new."

"Yes, it was a present from my grandmother," said George.

"Best keep this by you," said Thomas and tucked it into the inside pocket of George's jacket.

Thomas led George from the room, he paused and pointed at the next door on the landing, and said, "This is where the girls sleep, we're not allowed in there." Down to the next landing where two more doors that were closed, Thomas again paused and pointed to one door, and said, "Mistress and Mr Evans live here, and you must never go in. And here," pointing to the next, "Lives Master Gugiud."

Thomas led the way down the next flight of stairs which George recognised as the hallway he first entered into, and once again, down narrow steps into the kitchen.

George was met with a scene of organised chaos, the girls were placing bowls and spoons onto the table, and the room was filled with warmth and smells of cooking. Thomas pointed to a row of wooden pegs on the wall by the door and guested for George to hang his coat, and then pointed to a chair. Mistress Evans turned and placed a large porcelain Turin in the centre of the table which was steaming along with a plate full of thick cut bread. George suddenly realised he hadn't eaten since that morning and became very hungry, and all at once, everyone was seated. Mistress Evans sat at the head of the table, putting her hands together, bowing her head, everyone at the table did likewise and said, "For what we are about to receive, may we truly be thankful." As soon as she had finished, the table erupted with hands grabbing for chunks of bread. Mistress Evans stood and began ladling hot chicken stew into bowls. As she reached George she announced, "This is George and he has joined us today." No one said anything, too busy focussing on the food. "In future, George, you will wash and change in the yard before supper." George nodded, she then guested at the table and said, "You best be quick."

The kitchen door opened and the room froze, there stood the man in black George had seen in the street.

"Good day to you, Mistress Evans."

"Good day, Mr Gugiud," she said as she stood.

"And what fine fare do we have this very evening?" he said.

"A chicken stew, Mr Gugiud."

"Ah, the very thing to build strong young bodies." Nobody moved. "And who, pray, do we have here?" the man said, looking at George.

"I'm George Alfred Watkins, sir."

"Well, well, well, George Alfred Watkins." A crooked smile appeared at his lips. "Welcome to our family. I'm Mr Gugiud, the master of the house here at this home, and as it states at the entrance, 'our doors are always open, and no destitute child will ever be refused'. Welcome indeed," he said loudly, in an accent George had not heard before.

He turned once again to Mistress Evans and said, "I shall be dinning out this evening, Mistress Evans, and returning late, so I shall not require supper."

"Very good, Mr Gugiud."

With that, the master left, and the room breathed once more and went back to the task of eating.

On finishing supper, the girls helped Mistress Evans clear the table and wash dishes, the boys were sent to the yard to clear away the paraphernalia used to wash away that day's work.

Thomas introduced George to the other boys. One was younger than Thomas, one slightly older and the other was much older, they all nodded but said nothing. George felt that they weren't being rude but there was a defiant lack of enthusiasm. Thomas pointed out to George the coal shed, which brought back memories of his village, it was the wash house. "In winter, we wash in there," he said. "And here is the toilet."

"What if I want to go in the night?" said George.

"There's a chamber pot under your bed," said Thomas. "But make sure you pee into it first before you do anything else."

"Why?" said George.

"So you don't have to scrape your own shit off the bottom, isn't it?" said Thomas, the other boys chuckled. George felt a little better that he had made them laugh.

Mistress Evans appeared at the door. "Stop larking about. Chores done?"

"Yes, Mistress Evans," came a chorus of response from the boys. She handed the lanterns to the oldest boy and girl, lit them and everyone filed upstairs to their quarters.

George got undressed and put his night gown on, he folded his clothes and placed them on the locker beside his bed, he then slid into bed and pulled the covers up tight under his chin.

The lantern was extinguished and the evening light faded to be replaced by a low glow coming in through the window from the street below. This puzzled George for the next few hours because, the village he had come from, when it got dark, it was dark until the early light. George waited until he was sure the other boys were sound asleep, snoring and making grunts which restless sleep brought. George slipped from his bed without making a sound, the floorboards felt cold beneath his feet and he tip-toed to the window, pulling to one side the material strung across it, George peered out to see there was a low orange glow illuminating the street coming from gas lamps atop of poles at an equal distance apart. There was another light below him that seemed brighter and lit the steps leading to the front door. George stayed for some time, just gazing at the scene before he tip-toed back to bed and pulled the covers back over him, it had been a big day and he was tired but fought the urge to sleep.

Sheer fatigue must have gotten the better of him as he was jolted awake by a noise he had now come to recognise. The front door slammed shut, someone stumbling, more stairs being climbed and a second door being slammed, and the house fell silent again.

George was woken with a shake by Thomas. "Up you get, George, and grab your piss pot." The other boys were now stirring, they had been woken by Mistress Evans moments before opening the door but George had been so fast asleep, he hadn't heard this. All filled out piss pots in hands, the oldest leading the way taking with him the lantern, all still dressed in night gowns. They were met on the landing by the girls in a similar formation.

Out into the courtyard, they all tipped, first emptying their chamber pots. George had nothing to empty, and on seeing this, Thomas asked why he had brought it. George felt a little embarrassed at this. They all went about the morning routine of washing themselves, the older girls helping the younger girls and all the time protecting their dignity by bathing beneath their night gowns.

Once washed, they filed back upstairs to get dressed, Mistress Evans preparing breakfast, said as they went by, "Keep the noise down on the landings."

On returning to their rooms, it seemed that there was a race on to get dressed and back down to the kitchen to eat. George pulled on his jacket, saw the label still attached to his lapel and was reluctant to remove it. It felt as though this was somehow a 'no going back' final act, and he thought to himself, *I'll keep it and the ticket, it got him here, perhaps it would get me back again one day,* and he tucked them both into his bag.

A similar scene at breakfast as there had been at supper the night before. The girls hurriedly putting out bowls and spoons. The girls, this time, wore bright summer dresses, again, grace was said and bowls of hot porridge were eagerly consumed.

Everything was washed and put away with military speed and precision.

They were shooed into the courtyard to 'take the air' and walk off breakfast. Some of the children then joined them, having returned to their rooms to collect bibles. They were shortly joined by Mistress Evans and her husband, the man who had brought George from the station. Mistress Evans had changed from her maid's uniform, and was now dressed very smartly and looked very nice. Her husband, on the other hand, not that much better dressed from the previous day when he and George first met.

Mistress Evans set about fussing over the girls and bonnets were placed on heads, hair being swept up and under, and ribbons tied beneath chins. "And that's that," she proclaimed. "Let us be off."

They left the courtyard, single file, this time, Mistress Evans at the head of the girls and her husband at the head of the boys.

"Where are we going?" asked George of Thomas.

"It's Sunday, George, we're off to church."

As they walked, George looked at the street lamps that had him transfixed the night before and they were out. *How?* he thought, but, of course, they were, it was day light.

They walked on a couple of blocks, George struggling to keep up at the back of the line and there at the end of the street stood a group of people outside of the church. Made up of family's talking, they seemed to fall silent as they approached. George had been to church before but only on special occasions such as harvest festivals and the like, and he had quite enjoyed them.

The congregation now stood silent, waiting. There then came a procession of smart looking buggies drawn by healthy looking horses from which fine looking family's dismounted and walked directly up the stairs of the church to be greeted by the vicar who eagerly shook hand as gentlemen and ladies removed hats and filed in, pushing children in front of them. Once done, the rest of the congregation followed suit and then 'they' brought up the rear.

The church was dark, and by the time George's eyes had adjusted, everyone was seated. They were ushered into seats at the back, boys on one side, girls on the other.

The man of religion took to the pulpit and began his sermon. At times, George felt the man must be quite angry from the tone of his voice. George's mind wandered, and he looked at the decor and paintings on the walls, all of which seemed to predict fire and brimstone. George had no idea what the man was saying, and frankly, he didn't care, there then came a hymn. George recalled the visit to church in his home village and these seemed that much more joist.

Toward the end of proceedings, there appeared two people at either side of the congregation, plates in hand. As George was the last in, the plate was first handed to him. His first thought was, *Are we eating?* And he was quickly promoted to pass the plate along. It finally reached Mistress Evans at the end of the pew, and she reached into her purse and placed some coins onto the plate and passed it on to the next row of people who did the same. George was suddenly struck with the realisation that people were paying for this.

On returning to the home, there followed a series of cleaning task and the children were allowed into the yard to 'take the air' as Mistress Evans would say. The girls played skipping games, and the boys sat and talked. Mostly, the older boy, David, and he talked about how he was going to make his fame and fortune in a place called London. "It's where you have to go to make it," he said. They had supper and off to bed they went.

Monday morning came and George, this time, was awake when Mistress Evans woke everyone in the house. They went through the usual routine of washing, breakfast and getting dressed but, this time, work clothes were donned. Mistress Evans stuffed a sandwich wrapped in paper into their jacket pockets one by one. As they passed, she said, "Have a good day."

Each boy responded, "Thank you, Mistress Evans."

'Muck Boy'

George and the rest of the boys gathered outside of the home on the street, and at seven am sharp and from around the corner, came a large cart drawn by two horses. At the reins was 'Mr Muck'. This man not only had an accent George had never heard before but a language George found difficult to understand. George found out later in the day that the muck man had originally came over from an island where there wasn't much to eat, and found his fame and fortune in Cardiff. The boys clambered onto the back of the cart and they were off.

In 1902, Cardiff City Centre began to run electric trams for the first time, which people either embraced and enjoyed or hated and viewed with suspicion or simple couldn't afford to ride on. However, it would be many years before there was a complete phasing out of horse-drawn vehicles such as delivery carts and the buggies of the well-to-do, and thus, the recurring problem of horse manure in the street, so much so that the local authorities had commissioned the muck man to travel up and down the streets of the city centre in search of the alternative black gold, as the muck man would call it.

The boys were dropped off in twos in adjacent streets, George and Thomas in St Mary's. George was handed a pail and shovel with a short fat wooden handle that had already seen plenty of use. A shop keeper standing by the door of his premises, fists on hip and shouted, "Muck man, looks like you have a new fish."

The muck man looked at George and said, "More like a tiddler." The muck man manoeuvred back into traffic and clip clopped off.

"Right," said Thomas. "When you see a horse doing its thing, you wait until its clear, and you shovel it up and put it in the pail, all right." George and Thomas wandered up St Mary's, it was a wide thoroughfare with tall buildings on either side, all of which had shops of one sort or another on the ground floor, the upper floors looked as though they had families living in them as there was washing hanging out to dry and people leaning out of windows, watching the city come to life. It seemed all the shops had large awnings that the shop keepers were now unwinding, in preparation of the day's trading to come. The street was already busy with carts and buggies, and there was a tram but this had no horses pulling it, it moved on its own. George knew about machines, he had come here on one, but he was puzzled at this particular machine as he couldn't fathom out where they kept the coal.

People were rushing to their business, some in work clothes, some in smart dresses, and there were children in uniforms walking in line behind their mistresses. *Off to school,* George thought. There was so much to look at, to try and take in, George felt dizzy. There then came, from up the street, a shout that George would soon become familiar with, "Muck boy." Thomas's head jerked upward and ran in the direction of the call. A shop owner stood arm out, pointing at a pile of horse manure in the street, directly outside of her premises. Thomas immediately set about shovelling the manure into the pail, turned and doffed his cap to her, all the time George watched intently. It wasn't long before George had his turn, and as mid-morning approached, his pail was full, Thomas looked at the pail and smiled.

Just then, and as if by magic, the muck man appeared and pulled out of traffic. Thomas, with a swing, lifted his pail and turned the pail upside down onto the flat bed of the cart. George went to do the same, and found he couldn't lift the pail with one hand and struggled to lift it with two. The pail suspended between his legs, he waddled to the back of the cart, and with the help of Thomas, they placed the muck onto the cart. The muck man shouted to Thomas, "I'll be back after lunch," and as quickly as he came, he was gone, melting back into traffic.

Thomas looked at George and said in a serious voice, "Until you're stronger, George, don't fill your pail to the top, do you see?" George nodded, he knew Thomas was looking out for him, he had found a friend.

The sun was now high in the sky and Thomas said, "Right, that's lunch." They found a patch of grass outside of a church, wiping their hands on their jackets, they pulled the sandwiches from their pockets, and sat and ate with sun on their faces.

The day rolled on pretty much as it had begun. George and Thomas trying to be the first to the next pile of dung when they saw a horse lift its tail or the shout came, "Muck boy."

The final return of the muck man came and George knew it was the end of the day as the other boys were on the back of the cart. They sat this time in a squat position as the bed of the cart was now wet. George and Thomas flung their pails and shovels onto the back, and climbed aboard and squatted. The muck man seemed a little unsteady and Thomas whispered, "He's been at the inn."

As they reached more familiar streets, Thomas leant forward and said to George, "Congratulation, George."

"Why so?" said George.

"You are now officially a shit shoveller," said Thomas.

George thought for a moment and said, "Oh, I thought I was really rather good." The boys laughed so hard, they nearly fell off their boots.

A "Keep it down," coming from the muck man.

As they turned into Moira Terrace, George could see Mr Guguid stood at the top of the stairs of the orphanage examining his watch, a shiver ran though George.

As they pulled to a stop, the boys clambered down and scattered to the back of the house. As George was turning the corner, he looked back to see the muck man dismount and there then followed an exchange between the two man with the muck man handing something to Mr Guguid.

That night, George slept well, better than he had since he arrived at the home. He could only vaguely remember waking deep into the night by muffled sounds from the landing but this could not be right at this time, it was too early for morning.

So began the routine, wake, wash, have breakfast, work, wash, have supper, sleep, and on occasion, church. George had no concept of time, he didn't know numbers nor did he know of days, weeks or months, but he did know time was moving on as the season changed. It was now dark when they awoke and it was becoming dark on their return home at the end of the working day, and cold, it began to get very cold.

The house did have electric lighting, but only in the parlour, the hall and the kitchen down in the basement, and there was a lantern above the front door that lit the stairs at night. The turning off and on of these lights was strictly forbidden to all but Mistress Evans and Mr Guguid, and even then, they were used sparingly. Mistress Evans used the light to cook in the evening and Mr Guguid, late of a night, when he had visitors.

George was in absolutely awe of this new fan dangled trickery, and on occasion, Mr Evans would allow him to turn the light on in the kitchen only to then be scolded by Mistress Evans for turning it repeatedly on and off. "You'll break it, you silly boy," she would shout.

George could not understand how he could look at the switch, flick it and the light would be there quicker than he could turn his head. George had a secret, on the very few occasions, when there was no one around, George would go to the kitchen and play with the switch, on off, on off. He never got tired of it, but never in the parlour, there was something that scared George about the parlour and he would physically swerve away from the door when walking down the corridor.

Despite the house having electric light, the only heat came from coal fires. One in the parlour and a smaller one in the kitchen, George didn't know whether there were fire places in Mistress Evans' room or in Mr Guguid's and didn't want to know. These fires were lit during the day so some warmth did come up the stair by the time they went to bed but the house was perishing cold in the morning. George now came to understand the urgency of getting washed and dressed first thing, taking some comfort from the warmth in the kitchen whilst having breakfast before out they went onto the streets for the day.

The cold would bring a new found urgency to the game of being the first to the dung that fell into the street. George and Thomas would stand with one eye on the street and one eye on each other, and as soon as a horse lifted its tail or the shout came, "Muck boy," they would run full pelt in that direction, George being small but also, by now quick on his feet, would invariably beat Thomas to the prize. George would place the pail down, shovel inside and carefully picking up the rounded dung so not to break it, and he would cup it in his hands for it was warm and gave a brief respite from the biting cold. Thomas would arrive just behind him, shoulders slumped as he knew he'd been fairly beaten once again. George would always offer his friend a chance of a quick warmth, and would drop the dung into his palm and cup his hands around his friends and the boys would stand for a while and smile at each other. "Thomas," George said, "are we paid for this work?" He was recalling the meeting he had first seen between the muck man and Mr Guguid and many like it since.

"Well, of course," Thomas said.

"Well, when do we get it?"

Thomas laughed. "It goes to your keep, George."

There were other patterns to life that weren't as comforting as holding warm dung. George came to know the comings and goings of Mr Guguid. George was thankful he had nothing very much to do with the day-to-day running of the home and even less with the children or so he thought. Mr Gugiud would always be dressed in the same clothes, and would only be seen during the day, meeting with trades' people, delivering stores to the front of the house or the likes of Mr Muck, but George knew when Mr Gugiud would leave the house of an evening, which was most evenings, returning very late. If Mr Gugiud was to return with company, the lantern would be switched on, illuminating the stairs below George's window. He would hear the hooves of the horses and the wheels of a buggy on cobbles. There would be muffled voices from the street and footsteps up to the door, but on these occasions, the door would be opened and closed quietly as opposed to being slammed. There would be voices and laughter from the parlour below.

It was on nights such as this, George would hear the footsteps on the stairs of Mr Guguid, he knew it wasn't Mistress Evans, he knew the sound of her foot fall. The steps would stop at the top of the stairs and a door opened, it was obvious it was the girls' door. There would be the sound of muffled voices, one of which was definitely a girl's but he couldn't tell which one, they would descend and all would fall quite again.

A Dandy About Town

Mr Guguid was English and hailed from London, he was despatched from the capital to Cardiff to set up and run one of the first home for vulnerable children at the turn of the century. He was not best pleased to be sent to what he considered to be the ass of the country, but at the time, had not much say in the matter and felt loathed to leave a lifestyle to which he had become accustomed and to which, he thoroughly deserved. *Oh well,* he thought, *best make the most of it,* as he travelled up by train.

He found and rented 15 Moira Terrace not far from the city centre, and engaged Mistress Evans and her husband as house keeper and odd jobs' man. He had employed them as Mistress Evans had some experience, and was in desperate need of work and accommodation, but he also knew he could control them. Homes of this nature, although not established for very long, had already gained a reputation for taking in the waifs and strays of this land, and it would seem they had not only hit upon a much-needed service but a very lucrative venture to boot.

The organisation had already written to local parishes and those in outlying regions of Wales to offer their service, so it wasn't long before 15 Moira Terrace received its first children. They could cater for sixteen children both boys and girls up to the age of fifteen.

Mr Guguid received a wage and an allowance for the day-to-day running of the home. He was given free rein to engage local services and suppliers with the understanding he was to seek the very best of deals.

Mr Guguid looked, for all intense and purpose, a little out of place in 1900s Cardiff, his dress and mannerisms somewhat flamboyant, but he revelled in it. People would smirk and roll their eyes whenever they saw him coming, but always behind his back, never to his face, not that this man frightened them physically, but because he did hold some authority, and more importantly, the purse strings.

Mr Guguid was not a fighter, he had not the stature nor the demeanour of a man that you would be threatened by, and he himself viewed violence as vulgar and beneath him. However, he was no push-over and would not be taken advantage of. Unskilled in the arts of pugilism, Mr Guguid resorted to another form of protection, the cane he carried. From the casual glance, it would appear like any other fancy gentleman's walking cane, a silver tip, long black shiny shaft and a large round silver knob at its head. This knob usually came hollow, and Mr Guguid had this remove and filled with molten lead, on solidifying and once cooled, it was reattached to the cane, turning it into a very effective cudgel.

One evening, Mr Guguid found himself in one of the city centre dives having to rub shoulders with the local working 'scum', but it was there he would find trades people and strike new deals of supply. He needed these new partnerships on a regular basis as he would regularly exhaust the old due to him not paying them for their goods.

On leaving one such inn somewhat disgruntled having not been able to strike a deal to his advantage, he passed a table seating drunks, one of which on spotting Mr Guguid, said to his drinking companions, "Look at the dandy."

Mr Guguid came to a holt, turned on his heels, slipped his left hand into his pocket, lifted the cane into the air, catching it mid-shaft and placing it on his shoulder behind his head. "I beg your pardon," sir?" he said. The drunk, getting to his feet, staggered toward Mr Guguid. He managed to take two paces when Mr Guguid brought the cane from the back of his neck and struck the man square between the eyes. The man was stopped instantly, went cross-eyed and fell backwards slowly as if he was a great tree falling. His back hit the cobbles to a chorus of laugher from his colleagues. Mr Guguid tipped his top hat, turned and walked away swinging the cane and saying to himself, "Yes, I am a dandy."

Normally, the way things would work would be that the supplier, let's say a butcher or grosser, would have a standing order to supply a certain amount of produce to the home each week, were, in fact, only half would be delivered and profit from the other half re-sale split between them and Mr Guguid, the whole time the agency footing the bill.

But it was the other side of Mr Guguid life that he relished the most, his interaction with the city's holy ploy, the well-heeled and the well-to-do, this was where he came to life, where he was meant to be, where he belonged.

The upper classes would welcome Mr Guguid into their circles with false smile and weak handshakes. His parlour room manner was impeccable and they begrudgingly excepted his company, although to some, his mere presence was discussed among them, particularly the women. It was akin to one who was afraid of a spider, parallelised through fear but unable to tear their eyes from it due to sheer fascination that the creature held. But he knew this and took great pleasure in playing up to them for 'who if any held the moral high ground here'. He was tolerated, why, because Mr Guguid had a very special service to ply to these people, that of children, boys and girls, the wealthy it would seem, had an appetite that held no bounds.

Why the upper classes? Why did he not just throw open his doors to all? "Well, you see, the upper classes have a station, a place in society, they are hardly about to start boasting of such a thing whilst presiding over court or attending to their surgery, would they?" And all the time he could charge 'this lot' a pretty penny or two, just to satisfy their hunger.

They're Not for Us

It was like any other day, it was dark when they arose, they worked, it was wet and it was cold. The muck man dropped them off and Mr Guguid was paid their wage. The boys crashed through the gate leading to the yard, laughing and joking about the events of the day. George, as always, the conductor of this raucous chorus. The boys were halted in their tracks for there stood in the middle of the courtyard were three, no, four boys. They were huddled so closely, it was difficult to tell, that and the clothes they wore on their backs made them blend into one. George had seen boys and girls on the street who were less well-off then him but these boys that stood in front of him were literally in taters, and painfully thin, they can't have eaten for weeks. But it was the pitiful shame on their faces, they would not look up, they just stared at their bare feet, their expression said that they had given up. George sometimes would save one of his sandwiches and have it as a snack later. He pulled this now from his pocket, it still wrapped in paper and handed it to the closest of the boys. The boy, not looking up, mouthed the words, 'thank you', but he had not the strength to make sound. The scene and silence was broken as a priest came through the kitchen door. He was dressed in a long black gown, white collar, a gold cross just below and he was tied about the middle with a red core that dangled to his knees. He was being pursued close behind by Mr Guguid. The verbal exchange was brief. "I will not leave these children here with you a moment longer, Mr Guguid, and that's my final word on the matter, I bid you good day." With that, he shepherded the four boys out of the gate.

George found out later at supper that the boys had been brought to the home, and were to be taken in until the priest and nuns of St Vincent de Paul got wind and came to claim what was rightfully theirs. The organisation had a policy that they would not take in any boys or girls from Catholic families. "They're not for us, they have their own people to take care of them," said Mistress Evans to end the conversation at supper. When George went to bed that night, he couldn't stop thinking about those poor boys.

The next few weeks passed, there was the usually coming and going, some late at night. George, on those occasions, would sink beneath the clover and try to block it out. Winter had set in hard and the shops had begun to fill with all the cheer of Christmas.

George was asleep and dreaming of his stream back in the mountains, he could hear the water gurgling as it tumbled over rocks and he could feel the warm sunlight on his face, and there was his latest creation, a fine looking boat sat anchored by the shore, but this one was different. As he walked toward it, it got bigger. George suddenly realised this boat was so big, it could carry him, and he thought, *Carry me far away*. In the distance, George could hear his mother's voice, but that couldn't be right, why would he come away, it wasn't supper time. He then realised his mother was saying, "Go, George, you must go, go away now."

'Clip clop, clip clop' came the sound of distant horses' hooves. George turned to see Dinah stood there in a summer dress, her hair was down over her shoulders and she looked beautiful, she smiled and said, "You must go now, my brave little man," and she blow him a kiss.

Clip clop clip clop, George was startled from sleep, the buggy pulled up outside, voices. *It was them, they're back,* George panicked, *what had Mother meant, go, but go where?*

George's nightmare was confirmed as he heard the front door open and close softly, and voices coming from the parlour, but unlike before, there then directly came footsteps on the stairs. Up the second staircase they came, and at the top of the landing, they turned without pausing and passed the girls room. The door came off its latch and there stood Mr Guguid, he was holding a candle that cast shadows around the room. "George," he said quietly. "George," he said more sternly. He entered the room and pulled back the covers on George's bed, but George was gone. Guguid throw back the cover and curst. "Thomas, come with me," Guguid said without looking. Without saying anything,

Thomas climbed out of bed and the candle light faded as the door was closed.

George lay on the freezing cold floorboards beneath his bed. He dare not move nor breath, and that is where he stayed for hours until the door latch clicked once again and Thomas returned, got into bed and sobbed. George slid out from beneath the bed and he wanted to say sorry, something, anything to his friend but knew not what.

Morning came and as the boys scrambled to their well-practised routine, not a word was spoken.

George flew down the stairs and went to swerve past the parlour door but the door was open and a hand came through. It was Mr Guguid and he grabbed George by the collar. "Good of you to re-join us this morning, George," he growled. "Where were you last night? Do you have any idea how stupid you made me look?" Guguid had pulled George up by his collar, he raised his cane, aiming it at the back of his legs, when the front door opened to catch this scene frozen. "What's the meaning of this, sir? This is a private dwelling, I'll have you know."

The man stood there was dressed in a suit holding a case. On removing his bowler hat, he said, "Good morning, my name is Mr J H Stephenson, and I've been sent by the agency. I gather you, sir, are Mr Guguid."

Guguid's demeanour changed instantly, letting go of George, patting his ruffled clothes back down. Gugiud bent and with a sickening smile and said, "Run along, George, wouldn't want you to be late for work now, would we?" George needed no further prompting, he ran into the kitchen where Mistress Evans had been standing by the door listening. As George entered, she pointed to his seat and she served breakfast with lightning speed, gave him his sandwich and got him out the door.

"Mr Stephenson, please come into the parlour. May I offer you some hospitality?"

"No, thank you, sir, not if that's what you call hospitality," said Mr Stephenson.

"No, no, sir, you have me wrong. It is necessary on occasion to give a little show of discipline to keep the boys and girls in order, you see. I think you'll find my bark is much worst then my bite, sir, please take a seat."

"Pray, what brings you so far?" said Guguid.

"I'm here to conduct an audit on behalf of the agency."

"So close to Christmas?" said Guguid, a puzzled expression on his face, this was indeed an inconvenience.

"Yes, it's standard practice. End of year, that sort of thing, you understand," said Stephenson.

"Yes, quite," said Guguid. "Can we offer you accommodation, sir?"

"No, that won't be necessary. I've taken a room at the inn across the street," said Stephenson.

"Ah, very good, they serve an excellent supper," said Guguid. Guguid stood and said, "Well, Mr Stephenson, I have some pressing business to attend to. Mistress Evans can be found in the kitchen, and she'll be more than happy to give you all and any assistance. After all, our home is yours, sir."

Mr Stephenson stood and said, "That it is."

The two men shook hands. "It's been a pleasure, sir, and no doubt, we'll speak later." With that, Guguid grabbed his top hat and left, slamming the front door as he went.

Mr Stephenson found Mistress Evans busy in the kitchen. "Good morning, ma'am. I gather I'm addressing Mistress Evans," said Stephenson.

Mistress Evans turned and curtsied, and said, "That you are, sir."

"I'm Mr Stephenson from the agency, I'm to conduct an audit and Mr Guguid said you would be more than happy to help."

"Yes, of course, sir," said Mistress Evans.

Stephenson produced some paper work from his bag and said, "Can we start with the pantries?"

Mistress Evans followed Stephenson into a pantry as they looked over all the ingredients laid out on the shelves. "Are you expecting a delivery soon, Mistress Evans?"

"No, sir, not that I know of," she said.

"You run a very well-kept pantry and an exceptionally clean kitchen, Mistress Evans, it's a credit to you."

Her face flushed from the compliment, "Thank you, sir." She had no idea that Stephenson was paying her compliments to gain her confidents.

"Do you have anything to do with procuring the supplies?" he said.

"No, that's done by Mr Guguid," she said.

"There doesn't seem to be much here, Mistress Evans," he said.

"I do the best I can under the circumstance, sir."

"Yes, Mistress Evans, you are not at question here. Tell me, the children work, I gather?"

"Yes, sir, the boys with Mr Muck and the girls at a garment factory."

"And how are the children?" he said.

"I make sure they're clean and fed as well as I can manage, sir."

"And are they happy?"

"As happy as they can be under the circumstances."

"Good, good," he said as he examined his paper work. "And are they safe?" Mistress Evans' mouth had opened but stopped before anything could come out, she had not expected such a question, her head dropped and she stared at the floor. Stephenson placed his paper work back into his bag and said, "Thank you, Mistress Evans, you've been most helpful." He turned and left.

Mistress Evans sat face in hands and muttered, "What's to come of this?"

Guguid returned later that day and sort out Mistress Evans. "Is he here?" he said.

"No, he went out earlier and hasn't returned."

"Good," he said and immediately went about quizzing her. All she could say was he had asked questions about the supplies, and went on to ask about the children. "What about the children?"

"He asked after their welfare, and I said they were fed and washed each day, and he asked if they were happy."

"And what did you reply?"

"I said yes, of course." Guguid left muttering something about supplies and invoices.

George and Thomas stood under an awning, eating a sandwich. It had been raining all morning and now the rain turned to sleet. Jacket collars pulled up around their ears, George looked at Thomas and said, "I'm so sorry, Thomas."

"What do you have to be sorry for, George? You didn't do it."

"No, but that was supposed to be me, my turn," said George.

"It shouldn't be anyone's turn, George," Thomas replied. "We'll speak no more of it, George. We are who we are and we have no say in it. Now come on, let's go and find some black gold."

That night's supper was silent and everyone went directly to bed, glad to get out of the way. There was no sign of Guguid, and that night, no late visits, the house fell silent but there was an air of unease.

The following day would be just like any other day except for, at breakfast, Mistress Evans announced that there was to be, "No work tomorrow, children."

They all looked at one another. "Why, Mistress Evans?"

"Why it's Christmas Day, of course," she said with excitement in her face.

Later that morning, Mr Guguid returned to the home. Walking in, he closed the door quietly and went to walk up the stair. He had placed one foot on the first step and there came the voice of Mr Stephenson from the parlour, "Ah, there you are, Mr Guguid, could I have a word?"

Guguid eyes rolled to the ceiling and he turned, pulling on a sycophantically false smile. "Yes, of course, Mr Stephenson. I gather Mistress Evans has been of assistance."

"That she has," said Stephenson.

"And I take it, all's in order," said Guguid.

"I'm afraid not," said Stephenson. "Take a seat, Mr Guguid."

"There seems to be some discrepancy concerning the home's receipts for goods supplied."

"Really?" said Guguid. "It's probably a simple administration error. I do apologise, paper work, I have to confess, is not my forte, Mr Stephenson. I shall endeavour in future to pay more attention." And he rose to leave, making it to the door when Stephenson stopped him in his tracks.

"Are you familiar with a Mr Collier, greengrocer?"

Guguid turned, finger on lip. "Collier, Collier, no, I don't believe so."

"Well, he said he knows you, in fact, he said he supplied this home on a number of occasions with produce and you failed to pay him."

"Yesss, I recall," said Guguid. "He did indeed supply produce of an inferior nature and I recall we had words. I told him I was not prepared to pay for food that was rotten and riddled with pestilence. I have the wellbeing of the children in my care to think of. I'm sorry but this is just sour grapes, excuse the pun."

"Pun excused," said Stephenson. "Well, we have received a number of complains such as this, and I have to say, there does seem to be recurring theme here."

"Are you seriously going to take the word of these peasants over mine?" said Guguid as he lost his composure. "I'm sorry, I do apologise, I've been under a lot of stress recently," he said with an air of fain.

"The children in your care, I gather, are put to work," said Stephenson. "And we don't seem to have any records for this."

"Some chores around the house and some works of a charitable nature," said Gugiud, waving this off.

"I have spoken to the owners of the garment factory and they have informed me that they have been paying five shillings a week for each girl, and that you would collect their payment personally," said Stephenson.

"I have as yet to locate this 'Mr Muck' but I dare say, he will have a similar story to tell," said Stephenson.

Guguid fell silent, he was trying to formulate a plausible story in his own mind that would satisfy the man from the agency. But before he had a chance, Mr Stephenson said, "I understand there was an altercation a few weeks ago between yourself and St Vincent De Paul." No response came from Guguid. "I have it, on good authority, Mr Guguid, that your conduct here as a superintendent of one of our homes has not been one of a satisfactory nature, particularly concerning the care, welfare and the safety of the children placed in your charge."

Guguid now gave up any notion of trying to talk his way out of this, the game was up. Guguid turned and looked toward the ceiling, gripping his cane tightly and said with a hiss in his voice, "The priest, the sheer hypocrisy of it all."

Mr Stephenson now stood and spoke, drawing Mr Guguid's attention back from the ceiling, "I require a number of things from you, Mr Guguid."

"Such as?" Guguid said.

"Firstly, your resignation. Secondly, you are to remove all your personal affects."

"Today?" Guguid said.

"This instant, Mr Guguid," said Stephenson. "And thirdly, I have no doubt the newspapers will get wind of this, so I suggest we sing from the same hymn sheet, and say that we, the agency, and yourself had a confliction of views concerning the taking in of children from catholic families that had become irreconcilable."

"Surely, there must be some form of recompense, Stephenson, otherwise, why pray would I assist the agency?" said Guguid. "Because I am quite sure neither you nor the agency wish to see this become a matter for the police."

Guguid was beaten and he knew it. Without further word, Guguid proceeded to his quarters, and there followed a series of bangs and crashes as he hurriedly packed his belongings. Dragging these behind him, he paused briefly at the foot of the stairs, tipped his hat and with a sneer on his face, said, "Good day to you, Mr Stephenson," slamming the front door as he left, and Mr Guguid was gone.

Mr Stephenson summoned Mistress Evans and her husband to the parlour. Mistress Evans, her hands clasped in front of her, piny her husband cap in hand. "Mr Guguid has left our employ," said Stephenson. "You will continue with your duties as was and I will be taking charge of the facility for now until a suitable candidate can be found. Could you see to it, Mistress Evans, that quarters upstairs are cleaned as I shall be moving in today?" Mistress Evans nodded. Mr Stephenson reached into his pocket and withdrew some money, handed it to Mistress Evans and said, "It's Christmas tomorrow. Would you and your husband see to it that the children have a suitable meal and perhaps if there is any to spare, a gift of sorts for each?"

Mistress Evans was beside herself with joy, she curtsied and said, "Thank you, sir."

"After lunch tomorrow, I would like to address the children here in the parlour," said Stephenson. "That will be all," and Mistress Evans and her husband turned and went to walk out. "Mr Evans," said Stephenson. Mr Evans turned back to look at Stephenson. "Thank you, Mr Evans." Mistress Evans now stood, wide-eyed with realisation at her husband.

The children returned and washed and ate, Mistress Evans telling them that, on rising tomorrow, they were to wash and put their best cloths on, there was to be a visit to church. "And on return, we shall celebrate Christmas," she said. There was an air of excitement among the children and George was pleased to see their smiles.

The Great Escape

It was the early evening, and despite the excitement of the boys, they were all now sound asleep. George, without a sound, pushed back the cover of his bed, placed his feet slowly on the floorboards, put the pillow in the centre of the bed and replaced the cover. He had bundled all his belongings together and now lifted them in one go, tip-toed to the door, opened it and closed it behind him without a sound. He had practiced this for the last couple of days. Holding his clothes in front, he negotiated the two flights of stairs, avoiding the squeaky boards, down the hall and through the kitchen door, closed it and descended into the kitchen and waited for any sounds from above. When he was sure, he flicked on the light and dressed. He then went into the pantry, and found some bread and cake and froze like a statue. Had he heard a noise from above? Sheer terror gripped the pit of his stomach, what was he to do if found, what was he to say? The latch on the kitchen door went, and George exhaled with relief, for there stood Thomas, utterly confused to see George dressed and in the pantry.

"What are you doing, George?" he said. "Come away now, you'll be found."

"No, I won't, Thomas. They're all out, I heard Mistress Evans talking to her husband earlier saying so," George knew Guguid would be out on such a night and wouldn't return to morning.

"But what are you doing, George?"

"I'm off, Thomas."

"Where?" Thomas said.

"To London, Thomas," said George. Thomas now looked at the food in George's hands. "Don't worry, Thomas. I'll leave some for you all tomorrow."

"But they'll catch you, George."

"No, they won't, Thomas. By the time they realise I'm gone, I'll be half-way to London."

Thomas fell silent. "Come with me, Thomas," said George.

"I can't," said Thomas.

"Why?" said George.

"Because I'm scared to, George."

"But what's more scary, to stay here or to go on an adventure, come on, Thomas, you and me, we'll make our fame and fortune in London."

Thomas broke into a momentary smile and George thought he had a companion. The smile faded and tears welled up in Thomas's eyes. "I can't," he said. George had no time to spear, there had already been a break from the plan. He stuffed the food into his bag, looked around, saw a candle and some matches, and a small knife and put them in his pocket. On leaving the pantry, George spotted Mr Evans' great coat hanging on the back of the door, it was a heavy thick coat that, on a fully grown man, would hang about his ankles. George flicked it off the hook, and placed it under the flap of his bag and buckled it up.

George turned to Thomas. "Right, Thomas, I want you to close and lock the door behind me, all right?"

"You're really going, George?"

"I have to, Thomas." The two boys threw their arms around each other and hugged. Thomas was now sobbing. "Good luck, my friend, and when you can, come find me," said George. He turned and unlocked the kitchen door. "When you've locked this, remember to close the light and until they get a new boy, take my cover, it will keep you safe and warm." And with that, George was out the door. Thomas watched as George went through the yard gate, the two boys stopped and looked at one another's silhouette one last time, and the gate closed.

George stepped into the street lit by the lamps, and in their glow, George could see snowflakes falling gently. He could feel their tiny sting as they hit his face, he put out his tongue and could taste water. George felt a strange dual emotion. Sure, he was scared as he stepped out into the unknown but he was now free, he could breathe, all he had to do was find the road to London and get as far away as possible tonight.

George trudged through the snow, and came across a Salvation Army Band and Choir. They were singing, *Good King*

Wenceslas. George had heard this song before and he particularly liked the part where they sang, *la lalalala lalalala la* and stopped long enough to hear this.

He walked on for a couple more streets. Despite the dark and snow, there were lots of people around and the shops were busy, people preparing for Christmas. George stopped on a street corner looking one way, then the next. He had no idea which direction to go in. There across the street was a tram, not the new one but one with horses at the front. George approached, there was a man up front holding the reins, blanket across his knees, great coat, mittens, scarf and flat cap. George removed his cap and said, "Excuse me, sir, but do you know the London Road?"

"Yes, I do, boy, it's on my route, climb aboard."

"I can't, sir, I have no money."

"Well, in that case, you'll have to climb up here beside me."

"But I can't pay, sir."

"You don't have to, boy, it's Christmas."

The tram rolled on, and reaching a crossroad, they came to a holt. The driver pointed and said, "There's the London Road, now be off home, boy." George climbed down and doffed his cap.

George continued to walk on, he had to get as far away as possible, but the snow and cold was making him tired. He reached the top of a hill, and on the bend, he could make out the silhouette of a barn. George turned and there rolled out beneath him was Cardiff. He hadn't realised just how big the city was, and so much light, the snowy white rooftops glowing, the city was beautiful after all.

It was Christmas Eve, 1903, George was six and thus begun the long walk.

15 Moira Terrace, Cardiff, Christmas morning, 1903. The children woke bursting with joy, and went about their instructions of washing and getting dressed in the best clothes. As they sat down to breakfast, the children could see socks had been pinned to the fireplace, each one with their names on them, the children ate whilst eyes fixed on the socks the whole time. "Those are for later," said Mistress Evans. "Thomas, go tell George to hurry along, he'll make us late for church." Thomas obliged, he neither wanted to get in trouble nor give the game away.

Thomas returned. "He's not there, Mistress Evans."

"What do you mean not there?" Mistress Evans marched off in the direction of the rooms only to return with a grim expression.

On their return from church, the children badgered Mistress Evans to allow them to open the socks. The noise reached a crusado before she said, laughing, "OK, OK, open them." The socks were pulled from the fireplace, each child taking the sock with their name on. There were crayons and lasses and cotton bonnets, and the children set about making party hats out of paper and brightly colouring them. Thomas sat and stared at the one remaining sock on the fireplace, and thought of his friend.

Christmas dinner was of a like the children had never seen before, the table was spread with steaming food, There was meat and potatoes and vegetables, and Mistress Evans ladled hot gravy over it all and they could, within reason, have seconds. The whole time, Mistress Evans kept saying, "Save yourselves for pudding."

After dinner was cleared away, Mistress Evans announced that the children were to gather in the parlour to meet the new master of the house. The children looked at one another, having gone without for so long, had all their Christmas's come at once.

They gather in the parlour, all in line with Mistress Evans and her husband. "Good afternoon, children, I hope you enjoyed your dinner and presents." The children nodded. "My name is Mr Stephenson and I am the new master of the house. Mistress Evans and her husband will continue to take care of you, and your routine will remain the same. The girls will continue to work at the garment factory and the boys with Mr Murphy." The boys looked puzzled. "Mr Muck," he continued. "The wages that you receive for this work will be placed in trust for your futures, of course, you will be allowed small increments for the purchase of necessities from time to time.

"I know there has been difficult times but I now look forward to making this home as comfortable and safe for you all in the future. You are all welcome to speak to me at any time about any concerns you may have. Now back to your party, and a merry Christmas to you all." They all began to file out. "Thomas, would you stay behind please." Thomas stood in the middle of the parlour looking at the floor. "Thomas, where is George?"

Thomas didn't speak. "Thomas, I need to know where he is if I'm to help. I know you have experienced some difficult times here, Thomas, but I promise you, they are now over. Mr Guguid is no longer with us and will not return, you have my solemn word."

"He's gone, sir."

"Gone? Gone where?" said Stephenson.

"To London, sir."

"Oh, no," said Stephenson his shoulders slumping. "OK, Thomas, go and re-join your friends."

It would be a week or more before George's sock was taken down from the fireplace, and when it finally was, Thomas knew his friend was truly gone forever.

Mr Stephenson was sat in the parlour with a copy of the regional paper, reading an article about the former superintendent of the children's home in Moira Terrace, Cardiff, a Mr Guguid had felt obliged to resign over what he felt was inequality when it came to the agency policy to not allow children from a catholic background to seek sanctuary at the home. *Well, at least he kept his word*, thought Mr Stephenson. There came a knock at the door. "Come in."

Mistress Evans came in. "The new neighbours have arrived, sir," she said.

"Very good," said Stephenson, not looking up from the paper.

"I'm not so sure, sir, best you come and see."

Mr Stephenson went to the front door and stood at the top step. A delivery cart was outside and there stood beside it was Mr Guguid. On seeing Stephenson, he bound up the step of the house next door and removed his top hat. "Good day to you, Mr Stephenson," a sickening smile on his face.

"I thought I told you never to return," said Stephenson.

"How could I stay away?" said Guguid.

"What are you doing here?" Guguid stepped back, top hat still in hand, he raised his arms and said, "Behold the Irving Guguid Home for Destitute Children."

"How have you been able to do this?"

Guguid came close to Mr Stephenson face, so close, he could smell his breathe and said, "It's good to have friends in high places." With that, he replaced his top hat and tapped the top and as he left, his parting comment was, "It's good business, these children."

Mr Stephenson turned away in disgust and as he did so, he caught sight of Thomas standing in the street, Thomas turned and ran.

The Long Walk

George had made the right decision the night before, he'd been tired and the weather wasn't getting any better. He had found a barn at the side of the road, it didn't hold any animals, just machinery and a cart, in one corner was a large pile of hay. George unpacked the great coat, he thought briefly about eating something but it was too dark to see, and besides, he'd rather preserve his rations and perhaps he'd eat in the morning. He wrapped the great coat around and pulled armfuls of hay about him. He listened to the noises of the night but he wasn't frightened, he could hear an owl some way off in the distance and he was out, out like a light. George slept deep and sound, he couldn't remember waking once, so he was startled when movement in the barn woke him from his slumber.

From beneath the hay, George watched a man ready the cart in preparation of hitching up a horse. As the man turned, he, at once, saw the face peering at him. The man gave out a scream, George gave out a scream, the man had stumbled back and was now sat on the back of the cart. George later thought that if the cart had not been there, he may have fallen over. The man now clutching at his chest said, "You damned near gave me a heart attack, boy, what are you doing there?"

Gathering the man was of a good nature, George ventured out, hay falling of him in clumps. "Begging your pardon, sir, I slept in your barn last night and if I may say so, it was a damn fine sleep too."

The farmer roared with laughter. The farmer was a large man, he ate well, his hair was wiry and unkempt, large side burns, rosy-faced. He wore a heavy pair of trousers that were turned up two or three times to expose his boots, with checker shirt and a bright red hanky tied around his neck. "What's your name, boy?"

"I'm George Alfred Watkins."

"Why, that's my name," the farmer said.

"Your name is George Alfred Watkins?" said George.

The farmer laughed out loud again. "You are funny, boy. No, I'm George."

Just then, a woman's voice rang out, "George."

And both Georges responded, "YES!" George thought of his mother.

From around the corner of the barn came a young woman, hair up, dressed in a long dress and a shawl around her shoulders. "Why, who is this?" she said.

"He's George too," said the farmer.

"Well, hello, George two, and a very merry Christmas to you."

"He slept in our barn last night, Rosy," said the farmer.

"You never did," said Rosy. The farmer and Rosy looked at one another, and without a word, Rosy took charge and began to give out orders, "George one, clean the bed of the cart and get that horse hitched."

"Yes, my lady," said George one.

"George two, you come with me and help load the provisions, and we'll see if we can find some breakfast for you." Georges eyes lit up.

Not far from the barn was a cottage, he had not spotted it the night before and wondered why. It had a thatched roof and very small windows, and looked homely. In through the stable door Rosy went, she had come directly into the kitchen, the floor was made of large fag stones and a large wooden table in the centre. Rosy had been cooking as George could smell the air, so thick with aroma, he could almost taste it. "These are my daughters, George, Ruth and Helen." The two girl broke from playing on the floor, stood and curtsied together as though they had practiced long.

George, who had already removed his cap, and bowed in return. "George, you must be of a similar age to the girls," Rosy said.

"I'm not rightly sure," said George. By the size of them, Rosy was right, she guessed him to be around six or seven.

"Where have you come from, George?"

"I'm from the mountains, but just recently, I've been in Cardiff, Mistress Rose."

Rose thought about the expression 'Mistress' and guessed as to where it may have come from. "You can call me Rose, George, no need for mistress here. Do you like bread and meat?"

"Yes, I do," said George.

"OK, take that pail of coal to my George and I'll have that fixed for you on your return."

George picked up the pail of coal and surprised himself with the ease in which he did. George dropped the pail by the cart as George the farmer finished cleaning the bed. "We're off to see the in-laws, George, its only once a year, thankfully," he said quietly.

"George," came the shout from the kitchen and George was gone, the farmer watched with a smile as he scampered off. The table had been set with plates of bread and ham and some pickles, and Rose point to the chair, and George sat and began to devourer the feast. "George, where is your family?" said Rose.

George could have gone into the whole story but he still wasn't quite sure as to why his father had sent him away and he was to consume with the food in front of him, so he thought best just to say, "I don't have one, Rose."

Rose looked at him solemnly. "And where are you going now?" said Rose.

"I'm off to London," and George pointed as if London was just over there.

"For what reason?" said Rose.

"To find my fame and fortune," George announced, Rose smiled.

Rose left George to eat and went to her husband who was now hitching the horse. Rose stood in the barn doorway as George looked up. "I know what you're thinking, Rosy, and no," he said.

Rose came forward. "But, George, he's come to us on Christmas morning. It's surely a gift, George."

George, sensing now that his wife was truly serious, took her hands. "Rose, I know we haven't spoken much about our boy, but when we lost him, there was no one more heartbroken than I."

"But he has no family, George, he thinks he's off to that there London, as if that will do him right."

George took his wife into his arms, and said, "He's made it this far with this notion in his head, we can't confuse him now with the offer of a home and family, Rose."

"But if he excepted, George, what then would you say?"

George smiled at his wife who he loved dearly. "Why, then I'd welcome him as a son. Besides, it would be good to have another strong arm around the farm." Rose beamed and skipped away back to the kitchen.

George had eaten but was eating some more when Rose came back in. She stood beside George and placed a hand on his shoulder, and with a smile, said, "And how was that, my boy?"

"It was wonderful, Rose, thank you."

"My pleasure," she said. "George, what's really in London for you?" said Rose.

"I'm not rightly sure, Rose. All I know is I have to go and see what destiny has in store for me."

Rose knew at that moment that her husband was right even if she made the suggestion he stayed, he would always have wondered what might have been, but as a woman, she knew this was not for now, the be all and end all. "Have you had your fill, my man?"

"I have," said George.

"Then take this basket to my husband," said Rose. There was a number of return journeys to and fro with baskets of food, fruit and jugs until the bed of the cart was full. Rose gathered up the girls, George gathered his belongings and they all climbed aboard the cart. George one and George two sat up front side by side, and Rose and the girls behind. George the farmer had said that they would take George to the crossroads where he would find the London Road. They trundled on for quite some time. George the farmer relaying amusing stories about the farm, Rose and the girls singing carols from the back and George with the feeling that he didn't want this to come to an end, he liked these people.

Inevitably, the crossroads came and George the farmer pointed to the wooden sign, and said, "Look, London's that way." The two Georges climbed down, George the farmed knelt and held George by the arm, and said, "Now remember this, when you wake in the morning, walk with the sun on your left cheek." He stroked his face, "And after the sun reaches its highest point in the day, walk with the sun on your right cheek." Again, he stroked his face. Farmer George then hugged the boy and said, "Good luck to you, my son," and stood. It was the first time George had ever been called 'son' and that hurt.

Rose had climbed down from the cart, she took George by the hand and walked him to the sign. She had in her other hand a knotted-hanky, a lump of coal and tucked under her arm a hessian seed sack she had grabbed from the bottom of the cart.

Rose knelt in the snow in front of the sign and handed to George the knotted-hanky. "There's some food for you, George." She laid the hessian sack down and pointed to the sign, and said, "That word is London, George," and with the lump of coal, wrote the word 'London' on the sack. "Just match the words as you go," she said. Still kneeling, she flung her arms around George and said into his ear, "If you don't find what you are searching for, George, to be agreeable, then make your way back to us. You have a home here should you wish." She pulled away, kissed him on the cheek with tears in her eyes, stood and walked away.

George turned and walked in the direction of the sign to London. Each step, he fought with himself as to why he shouldn't stay, but he kept walking. Rose was now sat beside her husband on the cart and as they watched the little lad disappear at the turn of the road, George took his wife's hand and said, "If he comes back, we'll be here, Rose." Rose hung her head and George nudged the horse on.

The road came to an end and there before him was an expanse of water the size of which George had never seen before. This wasn't like the stream back at the mountains, he could barely see the other side. George walked past the large wooden post sunk into the ground. A thick rope tied about it that led down to the shoreline where a group of people stood and waited. George approached and asked the first man he came to what this was and the man explained that this was the Bristol Chanel. George asked, "How do you get across?"

The man said, "The 'flotman' would be here shortly to take everyone across." So George waited.

From out of the distant mist came a large wooden pontoon. There were men aboard pulling the rope between them that George had seen earlier tied to the post. Eventually, the pontoon was crunched into the shoreline and people disembarked as people readied themselves to climb aboard. George joined the line, and as he got closer, he could see the people ahead of him were handing the 'flotman' money for their ride across. Unless children went free, George knew he would be turned away.

George was next, and as the person in front paid and stepped aboard, George and the 'flotman' came face to face. With his hand held out, the 'flotman' said, "Money, boy," and the smile on his face told George he knew George couldn't pay.

"I have no money, sir," said George.

"Well then, you don't ride, do you, boy?" said the flotman.

"Is there another way across, sir?" asked George.

"Ya, you can swim," said the flotman, and there came a cackle of laughs from his motley crew behind him.

George looked down the river and then turned back to the 'flotman'. "Begging your pardon, sir, but how far is it until the river narrows?"

The smile on the face of the 'flotman fell away as he realised the child was being serious. "Pipe down," he then barked at his crew. "It's about eight mile that way," he pointed. "You'll come to a left hand bend where the river narrows enough, but the water's freezing, boy." In the previous two years, five boys had perished in that water, knowing this and looking at the size of George, the 'flotman' wanted to let George aboard without pay but he could not be seen to back down in front of his crew.

"Thank you, sir," said George, replacing his cap and he walked off in the direction the 'flotman had pointed. George felt no anger nor disappointment at the 'flotman', he had a business and the business needed to be paid for but the 'flotman' was true to his word, for soon, George came to the sharp bend in the river and in George's mind, it could be crossed. In years to come, the 'flotman man' went to his grave not knowing what became of the little lad he turned away that day.

George sat on the bank and studied the river for some time. If there was one thing George knew, it was water. He studied the flow and the movement, it was deep, that, there was no doubt but it meandered. He thought to himself, *If I get in over there, the current will carry me to that corner of the bend, but I'll have to be quick about it, the water will indeed be too cold.* It was getting late in the day as George formulated his plan. When he got to the other side, he would make a fire quickly, eat and make camp for the night.

George took his bag his father had given him, it had been treated with an oil inside and out, it didn't make it water proof but it would keep most of the water out long enough and with air trapped inside would float, well, he hoped it would, it had to. George stripped down naked, packing his clothes into the bag and fastened it tightly. *Well, now or never*, he thought. He slid down the bank and slipped his feet into the water, the shock took his breath away. He waited to adjust to the temperature, and soon, it didn't feel so bad. He pulled the bag in front of him and slid it into the water, and to his relief, it did indeed float, well, half-floated. It was when the water reached George's groin that he realised just how cold it was, and for a brief moment, George considered to turn back. "Come on, George," he said. "You can do this." He pushed off submerging his body and he had to concentrated hard on his breathing to steady it. He breathed deep and purposefully as he held the bag tightly in front of him and kicked.

Out into the middle of the river he went. The current had quickly picked him up and was carrying him to the corner, but George was shocked at how quickly he was running out of energy, the cold had drained him and he still was only halfway. He was filled with the dread that he might not make it, his limbs felt like lead, he lost control of his breathing, his head dropped and his mouth filled with water. At the very moment, he was gasping for air and he began to choke. George wanted to cry, wanted to give up, could he turn around, make it back to the shore he'd come from, fear and fatigue had creeped in and George had to steady himself. "I'm not going back, now get a grip, boy, and kick." The fear and figure were replace with anger, and George summoned a strength he didn't know was within him and he kicked with all his might.

George hit the shore where he thought he would, and as he did, he laid his head on the bag for a brief moment before shaking himself back into action. "Don't just lay here, you must get out." He scrambled up and over the bag. The bank was slippery and he nearly lost grip of the bag, and an amusing thought came to his mind that he would be left here in the middle of nowhere completely naked. With both hands and sat on his bum, he dragged the bag inch by inch up and over the bank until the ground levelled out, and he collapsed onto his back and sucked in air. "You're not done, George, get up and dress or you'll freeze," he said to himself. George first got on all fours and then pulled himself up, grabbing the bag, he tried to open it but his fingers would not work, they had turned blue and were ridged as he shook uncontrollably. He pushed on, he had to get clothes on and quick. Having finally got the bag open, George stood, and from the top of his head all the way down to his toes, he wiped the access water from his body and with every layer of clothes he put on, he felt that much better. The oil on the bag had done its job and his clothes were still pretty dry. George set about foraging for long grasses, twigs and wood. Having piled them together, he took a match, stuck it and barely able to hold it still, he lit the candle and held it under the grasses.

Soon, a fire crackled into life and George was suddenly struck with the realisation of something quite curious. Despite the fire, he had all of a sudden become warm, not just warm, he was hot. His face and hands were a flush with heat. George dived into the bag and pulled out the food he had taken from the home. It had to be eaten first or it would go bad, so George, having gather more grass to sit on, sat back and devoured bread and cake. George sat with his back against a tree, feet stretched out towards the fire, he pulled the hanky that Rose had packed him and unknotted it. He found a letter Rose had written, but, of course, he couldn't read it so he placed it to one side. There was bread and meat and three apples, and there at the bottom of the hanky were two shiny shillings. George rested his head back against the tree and said to himself, "I could have paid the 'flotman' after all. Oh, well, I need a wash anyway."

George repacked and tied the hanky, and pulled the great coat from his bag and placed the hanky inside and secured it. Using the bag as a pillow, George pulled the great coat over him and watched the fire's hypnotic dance. As the night sky filled with a billion stars, closed in around the camp fire, George for the first time felt fearful, but despite this, the day had taken its toll and George soon fell fast asleep.

George woke from a heavy sleep. The fire had long since died and before he stirred, George knew he wasn't alone. He moved slowly and raised his head, and there, no more than ten feet away, was a young deer, staring at him. She was beautiful, she shined in the early morning sun, big eyes and ears, she sniffed the air in George's direction. George wanted to reach for his bag and get some food to share with the deer, but as he rose, the deer darted off on her long gangly legs.

George gathered himself, drank from the river and walked to the edge of the woods. Looking up at the sun, George recalled what farmer George had said, "In the morning, walk with the sun on your left cheek," and George stepped off.

With each step and at the turn of every bend, George hoped that London would come into view. George was, in fact, about halfway into his journey, somewhere southwest of Oxford. George hadn't come into contact with very many people on the road and where he could, he would avoid doing so by taking to the fields or use these as possible shortcuts. He had, on one occasion, been chased from a field by a farmer or land labourer and as he fled, he had heard the sound of gun fire, not that he thought they had been shooting at him, more likely at pheasants. Because of this, George now had a strategy for dealing with fields. He would never use gates nor the entrance to a field, for this is where people would be. He instead would crawl up and under the hedge row surrounding the field, pop his head out the other side and watched and waited to see if anyone was there. He didn't mind if there was cattle or sheep, it was people and dogs he was looking for. Once he was sure, he would crawl out and instead of walking directly across the field to the opposite side where he believed he would re-join the road, he would follow the hedge row around the edge of the field and stay low.

George had now found a routine to his journey. On waking, he'd wash if he had made camp by a stream, eat a little if he had something whilst studying the sun and walk. He would sometimes stop at midday to rest, walk some more and by the time the late afternoon sun began to fade, he would look for somewhere to make camp. It was on one of these searches for a suitable campsite that George had ventured into some woods and found a dead pigeon. How it had died, he didn't know but it must have died recently as it was fresh, a small amount of blood that had come from its nostrils was still wet. George set about gathering firewood, piled up some dry leaves at the base of a tree for a bed, and away from the site, he plucked the pigeon and with his knife, gutted it and cut it into potions. Once the fire had got going, George sharpened some sticks, speared the pieces of pigeon, and securing and propping the sticks up at the other end with rocks, hung the meat over the fire. An hour later, George was feasting on hot food. George sucked the bones dry, and with great pleasure, tossed them onto the fire. George laid back on the leaves, pulled the great coat over him and stared up at the stars though the branches of the tree.

The following morning, George woke to find that a light coating of snow had fallen. He readied himself and although it was cloudy, he could still make out a hazy sun as he approached the edge of the woods. A few hours later, George was again in woodland and as he came to the edge, he adopted his usual stealthy approach. George crouched and looked out at what was a huge expanse of land, so large, he could see no end to it nor sides, and it wasn't kept as a field would be, the grass was long and clumpy. George abandoned all thought of going around. *To go around what? There was nothing to go around,* he thought. George stood and said to himself, "Oh, well, straight across it is then, probably save me hours of walking," and he stepped into the open ground.

As he trudged on, George became aware that his boots were becoming heavy with snow and he glanced back to see his footsteps in the snow. He smiled to himself with a degree of satisfaction as to just how far he had come. If George had only looked a little further beyond, he would have noticed the treeline from where he had come from had now disappeared. The snow was now falling at a steady pace and the flakes had become larger, a wind had gotten up and was driving the snow sideways. This time when George turned his head, it was to shield his face and on doing so, he realised the treeline had gone and he could now only see a dozen or so of his foot prints. The weather had closed in with a vengeance. George was suddenly stuck with a fear, he was lost, he didn't know what he was walking into and his footprints were steadily disappearing with the rapid fall of snow. "Don't panic, George, if you panic, you'll die," he said out loud. George dropped his head and pushed on into the driving snow, he thought about pulling the great coat on but he wasn't that cold. Just then, George thought he saw a form or figure in the distance that just as quickly disappeared in a swirl of white. He stopped and stared, waiting for it to appear again, and yes, something or someone was there. He picked up pace and moved towards it. What came into view was a stone wall, but it was rounded and short, about three feet tall. George could see it was in a horse-shoe shape and large flat stones had been placed on top to form a roof. George placed his hand on the stone roof and walked around, and on the side away from the drive wind and snow, there was indeed an entrance, but who would live here in such a small house? George dropped to his knees and looked into the entrance to be meet by a dozen woolly faces. "Sheep," George said.

George wasted no time and pushed his way in, dragging his bag behind. The structure was about eight-feet across and a large wooden-post in the centre supported the roof. Two or three of the sheep darted out, and as he made his way to the back, one of the sheep butted him in the shoulder. "Now, now there's no need for that. I just want to share your home for a while," and the sheep seemed to understand him. After a short while, the sheep that had left, returned and they all settled down. It became gloriously warm, so much that George fell fast asleep in the company of his newfound friends, safe in the knowledge that he had not just found shelter but also his companions would watch over him as he slumbered.

George was woken by the shuffling of the sheep and winced at a bright light coming in from the entrance, so bright, it 'fare cut the eyes out of him'. He grabbed his bag and made his way out, followed by some of the sheep who had by now become completely accustomed to him. George stopped outside, leaned back into the shelter and thanked the sheep for their hospitality.

The snow had fallen hard and heavy, and George was greeted with scene that was glistening, bright and still. The sky was without a cloud and a winter sun was at a height that told George it was about midday. Because the landscape had become so, even George still had no idea where he was and had to retrace the events of the night before. He remembered he had approached the shelter from the back so that must be the direction he had come from, so he looked in the opposite direction. *So that must be the way to go,* he thought.

George crunched on, the sound and feeling of stepping on fresh snow was very satisfying, and George felt good but smelt very much of sheep.

On occasion, George was glad to see people and it was on this day that George spotted a man sat on a cart. George made no attempt to hide or stay low but walked directly towards the man who made no attempt to move towards nor away from George. He just sat there, smoked a pipe and the two watched as they came closer together. "Good day, sir," said George as he approached, slightly out of breath.

The man removed his pipe, and from a face that was until this point stone-like, broke a smile and the man said, "And a very good New Year's Day to you. Where on earth have you just come from, boy?"

George looked back and said, "I don't rightly know, sir." He said, "But I do have some sheep for friends now."

The man thought for a moment and said, "You've walked all the way from there," knowingly. "Well, that's my land and those are my sheep," the man said.

"And very hospitable they were too last night, sir, when I could go no further," said George.

The sheep farmer laughed and then said, "Where are you heading, boy, on such a day?"

"To London, sir," said George.

Although George still had no idea exactly where he was and just how far he still had to go, the sheep farmer did, and after a moment, the sheep farmed said, "OK, give me a hand with these bales of straw and we'll head home. The wife has prepared a good meal for today." George climbed aboard the cart, and as he did so, the sheep farmer looked at him and said, "You really did sleep with my sheep last night, didn't you, boy?"

"Yes I did, sir."

"I can smell you from here," said the farmer. The cart rolled on down a rough track, back in the same direction George had come, and soon enough, George was reunited with his old friends, the sheep. George jumped down, said hello to his friends and set about unloading bales of straw. The farmer directed George to break and spread the straw bales across the floor of the shelter, which he did and emerged from the shelter brushing himself down as if he lived there. The farmer laughed. "Right, home we go," said the farmer and they rolled back in a direction George was happy with.

Soon, they came to a farm, a stone cottage surrounded by out-buildings and pens. George helped the farmer to get the horse out of harness and into its stable, and was fed and watered and with the day's work done, they walked back to the farm house.

"I send you, my husband, out to make those blooming sheep comfortable and what do you do, you come home with a stray," said the farmer's wife. George stepped into the room, cap in hand and felt awkward, but he needn't, as the farmer's wife was only teasing her husband. "And who might this be?" she said.

"I'm George Alfred Watkins, ma'am."

"He's going to stop and have some food, wife," said the farmer.

"Oh, is he now, husband?" sensing she was making George feel uncomfortable, she then beamed at George and said, "And you are most welcome, young man, on this day. Wash up, the pair of you and I'll set the table, I hope you're hungry, George." George would prove he was.

They sat to a bounty and having been told to tuck in, George did just that. A plate full of potatoes and meat, a meat that George briefly made a connections between it and the farmer but as hungry as he was, wasn't about to turn his nose up at and he did indeed tuck in. Over dinner, the farmer told George that he was still some way off of London, which disappointed George, and that he would be more than welcome to stay for a few days and help about the farm as the farmer felt he would have to bring the sheep in if this weather was to keep up as it was. The farmer's wife chirped in. "It would give me time to wash those clothes of yours. Where on earth have you been sleeping?" said the wife, and as the farmer recounted the story of George and the sheep, they all laughed.

That evening, George was shown to the feed store which was a secure building. It had to be and a bed was made up for him, compared to what he had endured over the week before, it was a palace. The next few days were spent bringing the sheep in off the land, checking them over, feeding them and putting them into a barn or pens, depending on their condition. George had been given some of the farmer's clothes which were rolled up at sleeve and leg to fit, and the lady of the house washed George's clothes which spent a couple of days close to the fire to dry.

George dressed into his own clothes, packed his bag and walked to the farmhouse. He was met by the farmer and his wife. "Right then, George," said the farmer. "Thank you for your help, you're a natural with the sheep, boy, you'll have a job here any time, should that there London not be agreeable." George thanked him, and the farmer's wife came forward with a big bundle of food and tucked it into his bag, and with a big hug, she said, "You take care, George Alfred Watkins." The farmer took George by cart to the edge of his land, and again, they said their goodbyes. In later years, George struggled to remember the names of the farmer and his wife but he knew their friendship and kindness had come at a crucial time in his journey, and would be forever grateful to them for it.

London

As George came closer, he had no need for the sack with London written on it that Rose had given him nor the advice that George, her husband, had given about walking with the sun on his face. The road started to become busy with traffic, and George was swept up and carried along with it. Tracks, fields and trees were replaced with proper roads, houses and then industries, large buildings and chimneys belching thick black smoke and people, lots and lots of people.

George had gone from purposely shying away from people to now being completely invisible to people. As more and more people appeared, the less they seemed to care or acknowledge his existence.

The streets became broad and George recognised the street lights he had seen in Cardiff, but this was different, this was big, this was busy. The buildings were so tall, he could barely lean back far enough to see the top. There were horse and carts and machines everywhere without horses, so much so, you had to look before crossing a road, such was their speed.

George walked deeper and deeper into this metropolis. There seemed to be shops of all kinds, selling goods George didn't even recognise, and people George had never seen before, not just by their dress but by their features. George walked through market places where people were shouting out the items they had for sale. At times, it sounded as if they were singing, he was surrounded by noise from every direction. A boy, not much older than him, stood on a corner, a bundle of papers in his arms and was shouting, "Anniversary of last ripper murder." George walked past huge buildings and monuments and statues, and the thought went through his mind that he had no idea where he was, what he was doing and more importantly, where he was going. Why had he thought he would simply arrive and there would be what he was looking for, and what was he looking for, he knew not that either. George now felt lost, not just physically but emotionally too. He had not been prepared to find a city so vast, so much noise, so many people, and yet, he felt totally alone and lost. George stopped at a corner and felt he couldn't take another step. "A step to where?" he said to himself.

George looked down the street to his right and there just above the rooftops was a flag pole, a union jack fluttered at its top. The realisation suddenly dawned on George. "That's no flag pole, that's a mast, a ship's mast." George turned on his heels, he had a purposeful stride to him now, side stepping people as he went, he could barely contain his excitement.

He came to the end of the street and was halted in his tracks, mouth wide open, eyes bulging. He was momentarily frozen to the spot. "Ships!" Big, big ships, hundreds of them, no, thousands it seemed, tall masts, rigging, flags flapping, guy ropes playing out a rhythmic tune by slapping their masts in the cool breeze. People hurriedly carrying goods from ship to shore, cranes were lifting barrels in cargo nets onto the quayside, people pushing barrows and big horses straining to pull carts piled high and heavy with cargo.

George noticed that there were also machine ships, bellowing out thick black smoke, and in his mind, he dismissed these as ugly, dirty and noisy and had no care for them. It was the tall ships he found beautiful and as he walked along the quay, he couldn't take his eyes from them. As he approached the next, some boys came running up from behind and one of them knocked George's cap from his head, and they laughed and jeered as they ran on past. George bent to pick up his cap, and as he stood, he found himself in front of the best looking ship he had seen thus far. She was long, three tall masts totally made of wood and iron but unlike the machine ships, she was beautiful, at her front was a carved lady, her breast bare and George smiled, a little embarrassed.

George walked back to the gang plank and was so caught up in trying to take in all the beautiful detail of this wondrous nautical vision, he hadn't notice a man had stepped right up to him and was now stood beside George.

The Kathleen was built in 1866 at the Charles Davison Docks, Connah's Quay Flintshire, Clwyd, Wales. She was of wood and iron construction, a three-mast traditional full square rig clipper. One hundred and ninety-eight feet long, thirty-three feet wide, a hundred and forty foot main mast, her holds were large and fifteen feet deep, and even fully laden could reach speeds of up to fifteen nots and, yes, she was very beautiful indeed.

George was startled when the man said, "Best you catch up with your friends," as he nodded in the direction of the boys who had knocked his cap off and were now terrorising a quayside stall owner.

George removed his cap and said, "I don't run with those boys, sir, they're not for me."

The man wore white trousers, black polished-shoes and a long black coat that had two rows of gold buttons down the front, on his head, he wore a white cap with a peak, his face, although weather beaten, was kind. George, for the first time since leaving Wales, immediately recognised a Welsh accent. "What are you doing here, boy?" said the man.

George turned back to the ship and said, "She's beautiful, sir."

"That she is," said the man now admiring the vessel himself. The man looked at George. "What's a boy such as you doing so far from the valleys??" said the man.

"I walked here, sir."

The man laughed and then realised the boy was telling the truth. "How long did it take you, boy??"

"I'm not rightly sure, sir, but when I left, there was snow on the ground."

"And where are your parents, boy?"

"I don't have any, sir."

"Why have you walked from Wales to London?"

"To find my fame and fortune, sir."

"I'm Captain Williams and this is my ship."

"I'm George Alfred Watkins, sir."

George's eyes now fell onto the loaf of bread the captain was holding, and on seeing this, the captain said, "Well, after such a journey, you must be hungry, George. What say you come aboard and I'll get the cook to fix us some food and you can tell me all about our beloved Wales."

George's dream was about to come true, he was about to step aboard a real ship, one that was big enough to carry him away to adventures.

London Docks, 1904

One of, if not the busiest port in the world, a port that can be recorded back further than the times of ancient Roman. The port and the connection to the river and thus communication with the rest of the world of that time was the very reason London came to be, and came to be the capital of England. As life around the docks grew, and developed over hundreds of years its own character and style, the docks, however, danced to its own rhythm. The very soul of the capital as it were, life and the routines remained very much the same without change. All was dependent on tide, the high and the low, for the Thames can rise and fall by as much as twenty three feet. Tall ships of the day that had deep drafts would have to time their return to port to coincide with the high tide or would anchor up further down the Thames in deeper water and await their turn to come in.

Something else you would recognise on the docks, whether before the times or since, the huge numbers of men and women that had to be employed to run and make this port work, and work night and day. Because everything was dependent on tide, the entire port and port system, including the work force had to abide by the ebb and flow of nature's rhythmic watch.

As a casual Docker, you would report to one of the local taverns first thing along with dozens of other men looking for work that day. The foremen would pick who they wanted, their favourites would, of course, come first and thus your working day would start. You would be expected to work a twenty-four-hour shift straight, you, of course, would get breaks to eat, but on occasions, even this would be abandoned, should a vessel need to be unloaded/reloaded and turned around to catch the next high tide, it could take days and many shifts to get a ship unloaded and ready to return to sea. You would work a shift and then usually take the next day as a break day, and this routine would continue day after day, week after week without break, as the saying goes, 'time and tide wait for no man'.

There was, of course, 'lighters', smaller boats that could carry goods from ship to shore if the vessel was unable to get dock side and hydraulic cranes, horse drawn carts and barrows, but mostly, the thousands of tonnes of cargo would be lifted and shifted by hand in those twenty-four or more hours, half the time in the dark, a hard, heavy and most certainly dangerous environment.

Because the docks ran nonstop around the clock, a thriving town within the city grew up around the docks, a town that would cater and provide services to the thousands of workers night and day for anything that was required, whether it was a temporary bed, still warm from the previous occupant, a meal, a drink or even a woman. It was there to be had whenever the work force required and not just the work force, the docks had at this time become somewhat of an attraction to Londoners, particularly the well-healed who would venture in at their peril to savour the colourful atmosphere.

However, amidst this metropolis of 1904, a cloud had appeared on the horizon. There had arisen a feeling amongst the work force that had become a real concern to the main companies that held sway and total control over all the docks. The work force was complaining yet again about pay and working conditions, and had threatened to involve the unions yet again, a situation that had previously almost brought the ports to a standstill. More alarming was the increasing involvement of the Port of London Authority, who was simply using the situation to further their cause in doing away with the 'companies' that held monopoly over the docks and had so for many a year. The PLA argued that under their control, the ports could be run more efficiently and they would improve labour relations. They not only had the support of the Dockers but also John Ben, chairman of the London County Council, as a labour man he was lending a sympathetic ear. It would take the PLA a further five years to get their wish, and in 1908, David Lloyd George, Board of Trade, summited the Port of London bill, and in 1909, the bill was pushed through by his successor, Winston Churchill, the PLA did indeed finally take charge, but for now, all was to play for.

For the 'companies', it was utter tosh. If truth be known, the situation had nothing to do with pay and conditions, and everything to do with control and money for the powers to be. As for the Dockers, the situation was far simpler, liquor. In recent months, the shipping companies had collectively come down hard on drunkenness whilst on duty, but it went further than this, fines and disqualification from work for days at a time, if any man was to be found pilfering cargo particularly that of an alcoholic nature. The work force saw it as their God-given right, a perk of the trade if you like, to help themselves to the odd bottle of rum or brandy either to sell on or drink themselves.

The situation for the shipping companies had become intolerable, not because of the petty theft by the work force, but the organised criminal gangs that had started to raid the warehouses on mass. Thus, the companies had employed guardsman and detectives to stop and search everyone at a moment's notice which had riled the man.

The Meeting

Captain Williams had been somewhat surprised when he had been summoned to the headquarters of the East India Company. Their quarters, housed on the top floor in one of their large warehouses, built some one hundred years or more previously. The building from the exterior, although nicely designed and obviously well-built, hardly warranted a second glance, it was clearly a warehouse. However, on entering, Captain Williams was greeted with a scene more akin to a gothic cathedral. Rooms were large with vaulted ceilings, blocks of granite formed columns of support and the floors were made of large York flag stones. As Captain Williams ventured further in slowly to allow his eyes to adjust, he became aware of the sudden drop in temperature. *Ideal for storing wine,* he thought.

Captain Williams, not known as a man of a nervous disposition. jumped out of his skin as someone from behind him announced his name. He turned, removed his cap and said, "Yes, sir, I am Captain Williams." His voices echoed about the chambers.

"Good day to you, sir, please follow me." The captain thought it strange the man did not introduce himself. *Perhaps a subordinate,* he surmised.

Up abroad ornately carved oak staircase, the smell of which reminded the captain of his ship, the Kathleen, and went some way towards making him feel a little less uncertain. The walls were half-panelled and set above with obvious pride were large oil paintings of the company's fleet, past and present. The captain frowning only as he reached a picture of a steam ship.

The captain could not deny the last few years had not been difficult. He had seen the invention of steam driven vessels, and for some time, dismissed these as a fad, but as their introduction became more prolific and widespread, he had begun to see these mechanical monstrosities in far-flung ports. His ability to secure charters had steadily diminished, and subsequently, came to a holt. So it was with these thoughts and, *why actually am I here,* that the captain and his escort arrived at a large dark wooden door, and the man, without hesitation, knocked and walked straight in.

Still holding the door, the man simple jested for the captain to enter and announced, "Captain Williams," and he left, closing the door and leaving the captain stood in the middle of the room.

The captain was greeted with a scene of hectic conversation, none of which was directed at him. There was, before him, assembled a group of five men of differing age, all in good attire, the younger in the fashion of the day, but each he could see and hear were in possession of confident and business like professionalism. The captain turned his attention to the room, it was opulent, Persian rugs, chandelier and again, large oil paintings. Just then, from behind the large solid wooden desk the men were huddled, came a voice that silenced all others.

"Captain Williams, I presume?" The man stood and came to him, hand out. The captain shook the man's hand, he had a strong firm grasp. "I do believe this is the first I've had the pleasure sir, I'm Mr Johnston, representing The India Company." Mr Johnston then set about introducing the other men present at a speed that Captain Williams had barely time to record. What struck him was all of the main shipping companies had a man at this meeting, now he was confused and again felt uneasy.

"Please, Captain, take a seat. Can I offer you some refreshment, tea, coffee, a whiskey? We have a fine selection of wines, should you prefer."

"Thank you, sir, but I'm fine," said the captain.

"Good, good," said Johnston. "And how long have you been back in port, Captain?" said Johnston.

"A couple of weeks now, sir."

"And what's pending, sir?" said Johnston.

"I'm keeping my options open, sir, at present."

"Very good, very good," said Johnston.

"Sir, with all due respect, may I enquire as to why you have summoned me here?" said the captain.

The elder of the collective gentlemen tapped his walking cane on the polished wooded floor and announced, "Here, here, get on with it, Johnston."

Johnston stood, placed his arms behind him and said, "Captain Williams, can I have your assurance that our meeting and subsequent conversation of the future will go no further than the present collected and these four walls, sir?"

"That you can, sir," said the captain.

Johnston said, "We seem to have a slight dilemma on our hands which we feel you may be able to help us with, Captain, as you will probably be aware there are grumblings amongst the work force concerning pay and condition."

"I have heard this," said the captain.

"We both know, Captain, this has nothing to do with pay and conditions. What you may not know, sir, is that the whipping up of the work force's furry by the unions and the PLA is yet another attempt by them at a takeover. The work force are all too keen to believe what they are being told and our captains are frightened to take sides nor make a stand. We collectively cannot see the strikes of the past return."

"Nor can we be seen to be weak," said one of the other man.

"I don't follow, how exactly can I help?" said the captain.

"We have decided the best course of action is to side step this dammed poor show altogether and allow it to run its course and thus fade away. However, in the meantime, business must continue and we would like to higher your services, sir, your ship and your crew."

"But why me?" said the captain.

"You're an independent, you do not have to have allegiance to any one body nor do you have to answer to any form of pressure from, shall we say, external forces," said one of the man.

"Captain," said Johnston, "can I assume your ship can be readied and made good for sea this very week?"

"It can, sir."

"And what of your crew, can they be recalled?"

"Yes, sir," the captain lied. Captain Williams had let all bar two of his crew go, but they weren't about to leave any day soon as they had nowhere to go, they had made the Kathleen their home over the years.

"But, sir. my ship is not equipped to carry coal or iron," said the captain.

"It's not these commodities we wish you to carry, Captain. There are others better equipped for those tasks, no, we wish you to gather and carry the more luxurious items our more discerning clients have come accustomed to and expect us to deliver."

"But we're not a steamer, it will take months, sir," said captain.

"Yes, and that's why we are making preparations now," said one of the men who had, at that point, not spoken. "We must be seen to be doing something, you understand."

"Captain," said Johnston, "we are prepared to offer a better than standard charter contract, considering the exceptional circumstance, what say you, sir?"

Captain Williams could not believe his good fortune. He stood, thrust out his hand towards Johnson and said, "I accept, sir," to a chorus of 'good man, Captain Williams' echoing around the room from the rest of the gentlemen. The eldest of the men banged his cane once again on the floor until the congratulations in the room subsided.

"Tell him everything, Johnston," said the man.

"Tell me what?" said the captain.

Johnston paused and then continued, "The Russians and the Japanese have gone to war, and the Russians have accused Britain of carrying, what they have referred to, as war contraband to the Japanese, it's, in fact, normal trade. However, the Russians have taken to stopping our ships and confiscating them, and only this week, we have had reports of Russian warships firing on British fishing vessels in the North Sea. The British government are reluctant to do nor say anything in fear of upsetting the Russians. All this has resulted in some of our captains refusing to leave port."

One of the men stepped forward and said, "But, Captain Williams, you have a clear advantage."

"How be?" said the captain.

"The Russians were able to see our steamers on the horizon from miles off due to the smoke they put out, you and your clipper should have no problem getting past them."

"That settles it then," said Johnston. "Captain, if you would be so kind as to return this office by weeks end I shall personally see to it that a contract is prepared and I will have all your papers in order." The 'papers' Mr Johnston referred to came as a buddle of charts, predicted course, letters of introduction, name and address of contacts, list of inventory to be acquired, an initial sum of money primarily for stores, provisions and port charges. Further sums could be obtained from a company representative who would be stationed permanently at each of the larger overseas ports. It was these representatives that would pre-organise cargo to be picked up and have this ready at quayside on his arrival, well, that was the plan. These sums of money could at the captain's discretion be used to pay for unexpected inventory, that chance encounter with a trader who just happened to have there and then a particular product that could be desirable back in London, but it could be a gamble.

The late piece of information concerning the war between the Russians and the Japanese had put a slight damper on what had been an extremely good meeting. Nevertheless, the captain was feeling particularly upbeat. *So what if I'm to be a pawn in their political game of chess, as they said I am my own man, I can distance myself from all of this nonsense, let's just get back to sea.* His thoughts then turned to crew, *Where am I going to muster a crew between now and week's end?*

The captain stopped at his local bakery and brought some of his favourite bread in which to celebrate his good turn of fortune. As he entered the quayside, a gaggle of noisy young boys came past him, up to no good, no doubt. There stood at the bottom of the Kathleen's gang plank was a small boy, he was just stood staring. *Curious,* thought the captain.

Welcome Aboard

As George stepped gingerly aboard for the very first time, he was surprised just how firm and sturdy the deck was. The ship didn't move, and why would it, thousands of tonnes of oak and sail versus four stone boy ringing wet.

"Philippo, I'd like you to meet, George. George, Philippo, he's our company cook. Philippo, could you fix us something to eat," as he handed the cook the bread. "I'll be back shortly, and, Philippo, we set sail at week's end," and the captain disappeared below deck.

At this news, a huge grin appeared on Philippo's face. "Hello, George, and welcome aboard the Kathleena." George found he couldn't speak for the vision before him, Philippo spoke with an accent he had not heard before, his skin was tanned and he had a small moustache and beard, an eye patch over his right eye, on his head he wore a colourful bandana, in his ears were gold rings, he wore a billowing white shirt and waistcoat, a large black belt and brass buckle held him in the middle. Suspended from this was a large broad knife, short trousers and one boot, for it seemed, initially, that Philippo had only one leg. In fact, Philippo did have a left leg but it was tucked up behind him, held by a loop of rope and he stood with the aid of crutches under each arm. Philippo spun and headed for a set of stairs leading down into pitch blackness. "Come, George, we eat," he announced.

Philippo was from Malaga Spain. As a young man, he worked as a labourer in the port of Malaga until, one fateful night, a barrel of wine came loose from its cargo netting while being loaded and fell some twenty feet directly onto Philippo. The barrel came crashing down onto his left leg; if it had been a solid object, it would have probably taken his leg completely off that night, but as the barrel crushed and collapsed on impact, so did Philippo's left leg. Both the tibia and fibula were totally destroyed beyond repair. The young surgeon who attended was reluctant to amputate the leg; it was a risky enough procedure, but for someone who had never attempted one before, he wasn't confident. The surgeon suggested they remove all the damaged bone and leave the leg intact as there didn't seem to be major damage to arteries, and thus, blood flow to the lower limb seemed to be good. Philippo, in time, recovered but had to come to terms with the fact that he would never walk again without the aid of crutches. Over the years, the leg shrank with muscle wastage, and on occasion, Philippo would strap it behind him, particularly in high seas to avoid it being knocked and damaged. Despite this, Philippo could navigate quicker around ship than any able-bodied man, and he had immense upper body strength, challenging all comers to pull ups, press up and arm-wrestling competitions whenever there were lulls. Philippo found other skills too, those as a cook and had become renowned among the shipping fraternity for his culinary delights.

Philippo grasped the crutches by his arm pits, held the railings on either side of the stairs and slid with a 'woohoo' into the darkness below. George left his bag on deck and made his way down the short narrow steps one by one; he had to, for soon, he was engulfed in complete darkness. From out of this darkness, he heard Philippo's voice telling him to stand and stay still until his eyes had adjusted. Sure enough, from the dark came gloom and then shadows. He could just make out movement from the room beyond. Once he had regained his sight, he joined Philippo in the galley. Philippo had dispensed with his crutches and had resorted to moving around the galley using rope that had been threaded through iron fixings in the ceiling. Philippo gestured for George to sit, and George watched as Philippo chopped a large onion and placed it into a hot skillet that sat on a stove and gimbal, it sizzled instantly. He then added salt, pepper and a good glug of olive oil; after a short while, he chopped and added a red pepper, and a good portion of Chorizo, Spanish sausage. All was spooned into two bowls, the bread broken in half and these were all placed onto a large wooded tray. Philippo turned to George and said, "Take the tray and follow me please."

George had to do a double take, and thought to himself, *Wasn't his eye patch on his right eye?* For it was now over his left.

George followed Philippo, who was now back on his crutches, through two further large empty rooms and he stopped to knock on the captain's door. "Come in." As George walked in with food, he was struck at just how large this room was. There was, of course, wood everywhere, floor, ceiling, walls, wood columns supporting the ceiling, large wooden desk, but just beyond the entire rear wall was glass, it was captivating, the like of which you would see in a church.

The captain had been sat at his desk writing. "Philippo, could you conduct an inventory and draw up a list of supplies needed?"

"Duration, Captain?" said Philippo.

"Initially, four weeks but be prepared for amendments."

"Aye, aye, Captain."

"And could you ask Jacob to carry out an all-points survey and report back to me as soon as possible?"

"Aye, aye, Captain," and Philippo left.

"Don't stand on ceremony, George, tuck in." George grabbed a bowl and some bread, sat and ate, how could Philippo have made something that tastes so good in such a short space of time.

After eating, the captain lit a pipe and smoked in silence for a while before he said, "Now, George, I want you to be completely honest with me, do you understand?"

"Yes, sir."

"Now, where are your parents, George?"

"My mother died and my father sent me to a home in Cardiff, sir."

"And you ran away from the home in Cardiff, is that right, George?"

George looked at the floor. "Yes, sir, I had to. I couldn't stay any longer, I feel sorry for those poor beggars still there, sir, but I can't go back, please don't send me back, sir."

"I don't intend to, George, what I'd like to do is offer you a job, George."

"A job?" said George. "But I don't know how to do anything, sir."

"Well, we'll just have to train you. You do realise you will be away from England for up to nine months at a time." George nodded. "We'll feed you, you'll get your own bunk, your duties will be that of a cabin boy and further duties around ship for which I'm prepared to pay going rate, what do you say, George?"

"I say, yes, sir, yes."

Just then, there came a knock at the door. "Come in," said the captain. The door opened and in walked Jacob.

"Good afternoon, Captain, is da news true, sir?"

"Yes, it is, Jacob, we will be back at sea within the week."

"That is truly good news, sir."

"Jacob, I'd like you to conduct an inspection of the ship to assess her readiness for open water."

"Aye, aye, Captain."

"Jacob, this is George and he is joining us as cabin boy as of this day, organise a temporary bunk for him tonight and then show him the ropes tomorrow."

"George, Jacob is chief mate and you'd do well to learn from him."

To be shown the ropes was one of the very first task you were given when joining a ship's company. You had to make your own hammock, fashioning it from thick rope and batons in an exact way, and of a strict design. It also had to be of an exact size or you could face punishment for taking up another man's bunk space. From this moment on, despite his size and age, George would be treated like any other man aboard, treated as an equal.

"Aye, aye, Captain," said Jacob with a big broad smile of white teeth. George had to be told twice, "Come with me, George," before it registered that it was he that was being talked to because George was fixated by this man before him, his face and hands were black in colour.

George followed Jacob back on deck, and they collected his bag and dropped this in the room beside the galley where Philippo was preparing the next culinary delight for that evening's meal.

Jacob and George then went back up on deck, Jacob produced a pencil and notebook and began making notes as he inspected parts of the ship, George followed behind and watched.

Jacob was from Jamaica and was sold into slavery as a child, he went to work on one of the large sugar cane plantations. One night, Jacob slipped his shackles and made for the only other place he knew on the island, and that was the port. He stowed away aboard Captain Williams' ship tied alongside the quay, there on one of the countless, 'Rum Runs', the captain had conducted over the years. It was three days before the captain came across Jacob half-dead with dehydration. The captain nursed Jacob back to full health, and from that day to this, Jacob never strayed too far from the ship and, in fact, for the first two years, Jacob never placed a foot upon dry land.

"Come, George, let us start ya education," said Jacob. "Dis 'ere's the Stern, the back of de bot, if ya told to go Aft dis is where ya come." George nodded and they strolled on Jacob making more notes. As they moved forward, Jacob stopped and said, "Dis 'ere's Starboard, it's the right side of da bot." As they walked across deck, Jacob put the notepad and pencil in his left hand, and with the right, he slapped the big mast, the one in the middle. "Dis 'ere's the main mast, I'll teach ya about de others another time, George."

"Thank you," said George, speaking for the very first time.

"Where are ya from, George?" said Jacob.

"I'm from Wales."

"Da same as the captain."

"Yes," said George.

"Did ya knaw him from before?" said Jacob.

"No," said George.

Jacob had obviously never been to Wales, and didn't know how big it was and just how many people were there. George thought, *Jacob probably thinks Wales is a village.* George would, in time, enlighten Jacob about his homeland, but for now, it was a time for listening.

As they reached the other side, Jacob said, "Dis 'ere's Port, the left side of the bot." Jacob stopped and inspected, and made more notes, all the time, George studying Jacob. They finally reached the front of the ship and Jacob stopped, put the pencil and pad away and said, "Dis 'ere's the bow, if ya told to go forad, dis is where ya come, da ya understand, George?" George nodded. "Ya a good student, George." The two of them stood quietly for a while, and just watched the hustle and bustle of the quayside and the penny boats going too and throw.

Lanterns began to be lit around the port and on ships, and Jacob after a while went from Bow to Stern to do the same, the gang plank was raised and pulled aboard and a washboard placed in the gap of the gunwale (railing) to prevent anyone falling overboard, and it was announced, "Ship secured." Later that day, George was given a locker in which to stow his kit, a hammock was hung and he was given some blankets. Jacob, Philippo and George sat on bench seats at a swing table that was suspended from overhead by ropes at each corner. George couldn't quite understand why they had done this, but it wouldn't be long before he would find out. Philippo had prepared a fish stew with potatoes and bread. The stew had some kind of spice in it as it made George's nose run and when he was asked if he would like some more, he didn't hesitate in raising his bowl. George would always say, "Never be shy when it comes to food."

The captain hadn't joined them this evening as he had paperwork to attend to and took supper in his quarters. While the galley was cleared by Philippo and George, Jacob took first watch. "What's watch?" asked George of Philippo.

"You'll come to know in good time, George, but for now, the day for you has been big and tomorrow brings the promises of an even bigger one. So, for us, my friend, its lights out."

Philippo closed down the lanterns in the galley all bar one and led George to the next door compartment where the hammocks had been hung. Philippo placed the lantern on a hook by the side of his bunk, turned it down to a low glow, stripped to his shirt, and with a single bound off one leg, landed in his bunk and went to settle. George, by this point, had also stripped to his undergarments and was now stood holding onto one side of his hammock which was at his eye level. George made a half-hearted attempt to jump and came nowhere near. Philippo rolled out of his hammock, hopped to the galley and returned with a wooden crate which he placed by George's bunk on its end and as George climbed aboard his bunk, Philippo held it still. "They take some getting used to, George."

George settled back and found that this new-found form of sleeping was really comfortable. Despite this, George slept on and off through the night, there was a constant drone from the quayside of people going about their business and also there seemed to be sounds coming from beneath the ship, sounds from the water. At some point during the night, Jacob came into the sleeping quarters, awoke Philippo, who then left and Jacob climbed into his own bunk, what sleep George did get was blissful.

George was woken by Philippo. He had no idea what time it was but he was excited to be awake and ready for the new day. He helped Philippo to clear away the hammocks and blankets, and Philippo said, "Take your clothes up on deck and join Jacob to wash up, and I'll prepare breakfast."

George climbed the steep stairs, and as he reached the top, the early morning light stung his eyes. He found Jacob on the starboard side of the ship where there was some privacy. There were pails of fresh water, soap and towels, and the two set about washing away the night's sleep. Jacob, who was now bare-chested, suddenly became aware that George was staring at him and he turned, and said, "Wat ya lookin' at, bwy?"

"Beg your pardon, Jacob, but you must have worked at the face for a mighty long time."

"Why say you dis, George?"

George took the wet rag he'd been washing with and began to rub Jacob's arm. "Because the coal dust just won't come off of you, Jacob." Jacob roared with laughter.

After a hearty breakfast, in which George drank coffee for the very first time, it was bitter and he didn't know whether he would drink it again, he helped Philippo clear the galley. The rest of the morning was spent with Philippo giving George a full tour of the ship from bilge to crow's nest and everything in between. Over the days to come, there was a noticeable air of purpose, people coming and going, making repairs, provisions being delivered and stored away. George was tasked with sweeping and mopping out the holds, quarters and decks. It was during this time George came to meet the fifth member of the crew, a large male cat. As George went to stroke him, Jacob said, "I wouldn't be doin' that, George, he doesn't take kindly to people." But to his surprise, the cat allowed George to stroke him.

"What's he called?" said George.

Jacob frowned and said, "Cat," and walked off.

George, tickling the cat under the chin and as he looked skyward, he said, "Blue, I'll call you Blue," and thus began a close relationship between the two.

George would, on occasion, sneak bits of meat from his plate and run off to find Blue to shouts of, "Don't be feeding that rat-catcher, George, we'll be plagued."

The reference was to the Black Death in England of 1348 when the plague was spread by flea-infested rats, we have come to know that it had more to do with the fleas than it did with the rats. Later in the day, the captain returned to ship carrying bundles of papers and letters. These were to be delivered to embassies, consulates and dignities at the different ports as they went. After a light lunch of bread, cheese and fruits, the like of which George had never eaten before, the four men sat at the base of the main mast. The captain, Jacob and Philippo were discussing the voyage ahead and how the preparations were going. The captain had removed his cap due to the early spring-like weather, when a seagull, way up in the top of the rigging, fouled itself, it must have had a remarkable aim as it hit the captain's bald-patch with a sound like a whip being cracked. George could not contain his laughter and almost fell over backwards trying to avoid the spray. Both Jacob and Philippo were now chuckling, and Jacob said, "It's good luck, Captain."

Philippo chipped in, "Yes, maybe your hair will grow back," and they roared. The captain reached for a hanky and George could see the captains shoulder's bouncing up and down as he broke into a laugh. George felt happy, he was in good company.

Captain Williams left the ship later that evening for a run ashore. He made his way to a local notorious tavern. On entering, he was shown to a table. Shortly, the inn keeper appeared and asked what he would require. "I'll take a plate, a flagon and some information, 'Inn'."

The inn keeper left and quickly returned with a plate of beef stew and bread and a flagon of ale, and promptly sat. "What's it you're after, Capan'?"

"I need to muster a crew, but I need men who can handle themselves."

"Well, then you needs to be speaking to Nafe," and the 'inn' nodded over his right shoulder in the direction of the far corner where a group of men were huddled around a table deep in conversation. The 'inn' got up, the captain thanked him, placing some coins on the table. The 'inn', before placing these into his waistcoat pocket, made the gesture of spitting on the coins and thanked the captain, and went about his duties. The captain finished his meal, smoked a pipe and drank his ale, and drank in the atmosphere of a lively but good-tempered saloon.

'Nafe' Nathaniel Fulton had been born into and had grown up on the docks of London. He started out as a labourer but soon found a more lucrative means of making money, thieving. 'Nafe' was in his mid-to-late-twenties, was tall and heavy in build. His career had started out with petty theft, that of knocking off the well-heeled that ventured into the quarter, but in recent times, he'd been responsible for cleaning out the company's warehouses. There was only two commodities that were easily lifted and shifted, liquor and tobacco. But, of late, things had got tough, the companies had hired gangs of watchmen who were prepared to stand and fight, but more importantly, couldn't be bribed. Nafe had considered moving down river but his face was now known, and on occasion, he would be followed by the companies' detectives.

The captain finished his pipe and tapped it out on the leg of the table. He stood, fastened his jacket and turned in the direction of Nafe. The moment he did, Nafe's eyes fixed on him and never left. As the captain approached the table, Nafe's hand slowly and subtly dropped to his belt where a large knife hung. "Good evening, gentlemen, my name is Captain Williams. I hope I'm not intruding."

"Not at all, Captain, what can we do you for?" said Nafe.

"I gather I'm addressing Nafe."

"That you are, sir. Nathaniel Fulton, sir, at your service." Nafe stood and put forward his hand. Nafe was not concerned, this was no company man before him. "You're off the Kathleen, if I'm not mistaken, Captain."

"That I am and I've come with a proposition, sir."

"Up, and let the captain sit," Nafe barked at the two other men sat at the table, who promptly did so, they then loitered by the table. Nafe looked at these two and said, "Sod off to the bar, the captain and I have business." Nafe asked the captain if he wanted a drink and the captain declined.

The two men engaged in deep conversation for more than an hour, culminating in the two standing and shaking hands.

It was now late as the captain strolled back to his ship, happy that he had secured a crew. The captain was at home in this environment, safe, no one in their right mind would assault a crew member, let alone a captain, in fear of suffering the wrath of an entire ship's company the following night.

The following morning, George conducted his ablutions after tidying away the bunks and joined Jacob in the galley for breakfast. He watched Philippo fill a barrel with fresh water and then add a good glug of white rum. Seeing George's interest, he said, "It stop the water going bad, George."

That's why it tasted different, thought George. Philippo sat and ate breakfast with them, George had noticed that Philippo's eye-patch was now over his right eye again, and after a while, George plucked up the courage to ask, "What's wrong with your eyes, Philippo?"

"Nothing," said Philippo as he flipped the eye patch up revelling a perfectly good eye.

"Then why do you wear a patch?" said George.

"I wear it on one eye or the other when I'm up on deck, so when I come below and can see in the dark with that eye." George couldn't quite fathom this logic out but he thought it was very clever and would try this for himself sometime.

It was the night before departure, the gang plank had been left out and under the cover of darkness, 'Nafe' and his gang came aboard. Including Nafe, there were six of them in all. Of the six, George only really recalls coming to know three over the voyages as some came and went. 'Nafe', of course, and the brothers, Horton, Albert and Edward. The brothers were close in age and fierce rivals in a good-natured way, they were a pair of bookends, who 'Nafe' would comment that "If they ran at each other and clashed heads, there wouldn't even be a spark." The rest were a ragtag bunch that thankfully kept themselves to themselves. They made their way directly below decks, all of these man having lived, worked of sorts and grown up on the docks, and thus knew their way around a ship and George for now would remained very much 'the greenhorn'.

The morning of departure had arrived. After George had taken care of the bunks, which took a little longer now as there were that many more. He inspected all decks, the bilge first, by lantern for any problems, he would give the captain his report later as expected. He would, as told, clean the 'heads' (toilets) properly once they were under way as he would then have a flow of water coming in from the bow break to do this with, the head was situated at the front of the ship and at water line level.

George could hear the galley long before he walked in. Philippo had strung up another swing table and had laid it with food which Nafe and his men now occupied, having breakfast and it was a noisy one. As George sat at the other table with Philippo, there came jibs and jives from Nafe's man, none of which he quite understood. Banter was a big part of how men in close quarters communicated with one another, it was sometimes harsh but never truly meant and you had to develop a thick skin if you were to survive.

"Philippo," said one of 'Nafe's' man. "Best foot forward, ah, mate."

The man laughed and 'Nafe' chipped in, "Don't worry, Philippo, he's only pulling your leg, mate, the good one that is," and again, the men fell about with laughter.

George's attention was immediately taken charge of by Philippo who slid a plate of food in front of him and simple said, "They're buffoons, George, now eat." This din came to an abrupt halt as Philippo announced loudly, "Capan on deck," and all the men promptly stood to attention. George, the last, having not experienced this before, something the captain overlooked.

"Good morning, gentleman, please be seated." George was the last again. "I hope you have eaten heartily." The men nodded. "We will be departing shortly. I would like to welcome you aboard, and look forward to a safe and profitable run, as and when we are clear from sight of the port, I will give your first mate, Mr Fulton, word and you may join us on deck and we will properly get under way." Some of Nafe's men tried to make fun of his newly elevated position and Nafe's put them down with just a look. "Good luck, gentlemen," said the captain.

"Shun," shouted Philippo and all the men stood as the captain left.

After George cleared the galley and cleaned the plates by himself, he hurriedly went up on deck. Philippo was already there in charge of the helm as the captain stood behind looking over the rail of the poop deck. Jacob was forward at the bow. George climbed the steps and reported to the captain. "All's well, is it, George?"

"Yes, Captain, she is."

"Join Jacob forward, would you please?" said the captain and George scampered off hardly able to contain his excitement.

"Good morning, George," said Jacob as he approached.

"Good morning, Jacob," replied George. "What happens now?" asked George.

"We're waiting on the steam tugs and they'll pull us clear and take us down river," said Jacob.

"Steam?" said George.

"Ya, George, da machine."

"Has everything been made into a machine, Jacob?" asked George.

"Yep, George, they say a man in the Americas has built a machine dat flies like a bird," and Jacob pointed to the sky. George struggled for a moment to imagine this, and to his mind, came the vision of a monstrous machine swooping in from the sky, breathing fire from its belly and black smoke bellowing from its nostrils. *Dragons,* he thought, *but not the good ones. Rail, road, ocean and now the sky's, was this world to become run by machines?*

A vision that seemed a little less threatening when, from around the quay and into the black pool of the port, came two short fat stumpy steam tugs that buzzed about the Kathleen like bees around a hive. George, taking direction from Jacob as ropes were thrown aboard fore and aft, and made secure, and as the ropes that had lashed the Kathleen to land like a wild horse tethered were loosened, let go, brought inboard and stowed the tugs took charge. Captain Williams shouted, "Fenders in." He viewed and held this part of the voyage with great disdain as his beloved Kathleen was as he saw it being manhandle and molested by these ruffian tugs. For the first time, the Kathleen moved beneath George's feet as she slowly glided out of port. Old men at quayside doffed their sea caps as children ran alongside the quay cheering and waving them off.

As all the industry of the port fell away and the river turned into an estuary, the tug thugs finally let the captive Kathleen lose. The captain gave word and 'Nafe' and his man came up top. "George, come stand by me," said the captain. As George was indeed the 'greenhorn', he would be best out the way as these men went about the business of getting under way. "Watch," said the captain as he approached. Orders were barked, but at times, didn't seem necessary as the men instinctively went to task, and working as a team, the canvas fore and aft were unfurled, secured and snapped to attention as the breeze court them and as they did, the Kathleen jerked into life. This motion caught George off balance, and as he looked at Philippo, he wondered how he kept his.

Philippo was the best helmsman aboard, bar the captain, despite having one leg, he would say he had a distinct advantage because of this, he felt a greater connection, empathy, a oneness with Kathleen, a love no less greater than the captain's.

It was spring, 1904, and we were under way.

The Kathleen stayed within sight of land and rounded Broad stairs and into the English channel. Again, a burst of orders and activity on deck as men scrambled up nets, and the main sail was dropped and made safe, there was a noticeable change in speed as the Kathleen pick up pace. For some time, not much more happened but all hands remained on deck, this was one of the busiest shipping lanes in the world and the captain needed all eyes outward.

'Nafe' made his way over to Jacob, introduced himself and they shook hands. The two men stood and discussed working procedures, watchers and drills. After a time, Nafe said, "The capan said this voyage may hold some perils."

"Ya never knows," said Jacob.

"Then, pray, tell me, Jacob, just how peril-less does a journey have to be, that we feel the necessity to have a pirate on board?" As he nodded at the vision of Philippo stood at the helm.

Jacob leaned in and said, "He's na pirate, he's worst's than dat."

"How so?" said Nafe, now intrigued.

"He's the cook," said Jacob, as he went to inspect some lines.

George stood on the poop deck and watched unblinking as England faded. The horizon, that line between sea and sky became all dominant as if land had never existed, and this became a ritual for George, regardless of what ever land they departed from and he knew not why.

Since the dawn of our earliest awakenings, man has wished, wanted, yearned and craved, some have even dared to concur the waters that they braved. If you could taste the ocean in your tears, then you were truly a man of the seas, despite your mortal fears. Like a mother separated from a child, always a wish to reunite, whether temperament harsh or mild. Moak.

George was finding it difficult to stand on deck, his legs had, all of a sudden, decided not to work and the more he tried to stand, the more ridicules he looked, like a new-born foal, its legs gangly and aquiver. "You'll find your legs soon enough," said the man with only one, and George, although he didn't say aloud, thought this ironic.

Mid-English channel between the Isle of Wight and Cherbourg just off saint Anne, we first spied the two heavy Russian battle cruisers. "Capan," said Philippo, although the captain wasn't looking in that direction, he knew they were there. He'd seen the wisps of their smoke on the horizon many miles back, that and he had been forewarned by a fellow captain back in port that they were there and thus he decided to sail directly for them.

"Stay the course, Philippo," said the captain. The course would take them directly across their bow's and although at some distant still well within the range of their heavy guns, but also a grange close enough for the Russians to clearly see Kathleen's water line and thus that she was empty and nothing for the Russians to gain.

On board the lead Russian ship, the officer of the watch peered through his binoculars at the Kathleen and somewhat admired the sheer audacity and braze-nous of this captain and his vessel. But it was one thing to attack a ship carrying cargo and quite another to attack a ship that was clearly empty. The officer still observing the Kathleen, said, "Make a note of the date, time and her name, we'll take her on her return."

A collective sigh of relief was heaved by the crew aboard the Kathleen as they went by unchallenged. At which point, the men jeered and flung insults in the direction of the Russians and cheers of "Good on ya, Capan, and bravo, sir," toward the poop deck. The captain said nothing and made no expression, but all the time, smiled within that the plan had indeed worked. *But what of our return?* he thought.

It was late and dark, as the Kathleen with lanterns lit, sailed into St Peter Port, Guernsey. There would be no run ashore for the men, they would drop anchor in the bay, lay up overnight and conduct a full inspection of the ship the following morning, for what was about to come would make the fear of a showdown with the Russian's pail into insignificants.

The men that night ate to recounts of the day's events, each one becoming more and more elaborate as it was told, followed by raising of cups to the captain, he had well and truly gained their trust and respect that day. The roster of the watch was set and George had his very first night at sea.

The following morning came, and the usual routine of clearing away of bunks and washing. After breakfast, George helped Philippo clear the galley, but this time, the swing tables were hoisted to the overhead and tied off, the bench seats lashed to the bulk head. Philippo then rake out the coals from the stove, he had earlier prepared dry rations for the next twenty-four hours. Anything that could come loose was secured, in fact, the entire galley could be turned upside down and nothing would move. The inspection of decks and rigging was carried out by all to ascertain how the ship faired on her departure, all be it a small journey, but if something were to be wrong then it needs to be early and in port. The next leg of the journey was and had always been that of a testing one, the crossing of the Bay of Biscay. In times before, the captain had set course from Brest in France directly across the bay to la Coruna in Spain, spending a good deal of time away from shore despite the legendary and fearsome reputation of the bay. However, this time was different, they were carrying no stowage, and in thick weather and with full rig, she would be toss about like a cork in a babbling brook. With this in mind, the captain chose a course that would take them from Brest to Santander and thus stay within easy reach of the coast, should the North Atlantic and the Westley's decide, at any given moment, to do their best.

With the 'all good' the captain gave the order, "Up anchor," and to bring them and all cables inboard as hanging on the outside of the ship would only add to the unsteadiness of her, they wouldn't break these out again until their approach to Gibraltar.

Gibraltar, that rocky out-crop of the British Empire, was some one-thousand-three-hundred-and-seventy-four nautical miles from England and in fair weather and winds was easily reached within a week. But the captain was not concerned with speed as other captains of the day seemed to be, he was more concerned with the safety of his crew and that of his ship. But it didn't hurt that he had one of the fastest clipper on the high seas today and she was known for it. Her speed and ease of handing with so few crew had been accomplished at the insistence of the captain's involvement during the design and construction of her in North Wales. People had frowned and scratched their heads at his ideas, but he had proved he was right, she was not only beautiful but fast and agile to, all the more reason not to put her at risk.

So George, for the second time and for a second day, watched as the land sunk away. He again stood by the captain on the poop and watched. Philippo at the helm, the crew went about heaving the heavy anchors and rig inboard and stowing them forward. They then went about doing the same George had just done in the galley, rigging and ropes belayed and stowed, hatches and portholes secured. The captain then assumed a demeanour and routine that George would over-time become accustomed too and understand.

The captain for minutes-on-end would scour the horizon to the West and then spend as much time looking at the sky, the rigging and then the sea. He would cast his eye to the shore and periodically disappear below deck to study charts and make observations in the log but would return promptly up on deck. For hours, this continued as George followed the captain who didn't seem to mind his presents, and in fact, George wondered, if, at times, the captain even knew he was there. George couldn't see what warranted such close scrutiny, there was a light breeze, there were clouds in the sky but they were white and few in number, and there was a slight swell but it was gentle.

Tell-Tales

Just then, one of the 'tell-tales' high up in the rigging made a whip crack sound. 'Tell-tales' were long strips of material, usually silk, that on a still day would just hang. With a breeze, they would gently flutter and with an approaching storm would let you know by snapping to attention. With the first crack of the 'tell-tale', the men on deck to a one frozen dead where they were and all gazed aloft, silence and then 'crack' came the sound again, and all at once, men were dashing in all directions making doubly sure all was secure.

Jacob came to George and physically put a life jacket on him and said, "George, da not take this aff until I tell you, OK?" George nodded. "Dis ere a lanyard," as he tied it around George. "Dis is the clip at the end of it, if I should shout secure a line, clip onto anything solid, George, do you understand?" Again, George nodded, and Jacob was gone.

What on earth is going on? George asked himself.

The man stood and watched as the horizon grew thick and dark, and the gentle breeze turned into a steady wind. The temperature dropped noticeable, but this storm is miles away. *We'll probably be in port by the time that reaches us,* thought George as the first big dip came from the bow, the sails began to flap, and on occasion, would collapse altogether only to refill violently. As the ship rose and fell, so did George, unable to keep his footing. There was no fun in this, and for the first time in a long while, he was frightened. As he held onto a rail and stared at the deck all about him became black, the light was snuffed out and as he looked up for the sky, the sky had gone, replaced by a coal black cloud that whirled at speed and came crashing down upon Kathleen. Hail stones the size of marbles thwacked into the sails, and within one minute, her decks were white. George made for cover under the poop deck and held on as gust of wind drove

Kathleen sideways, and she dip and dive once again in an ocean that was rolling to a height of ten to fifteen feet. George thought as he held on, *If she rolls much more, the sails will hit the water.* The hail had been replaced and washed away by rain all be it heavy but the men seemed happier with this. The storm roared and whaled at us as if we had trespassed against it, and Kathleen protested with groans and moans and shuddered every time her course was altered against her will, and the wind blew at times so strong and loud, you could not hear yourself scream, which for George was the only thing he was grateful for. On a number of occasions, he was told to go below, but the thought of this scared him more than anything. Besides, he dared not let go of the beam, he had thrown his arms and legs around. At times, the Kathleen was so awash with sea and rain, the view of the bow was totally obscured, but between, George could see members of the crew going about their tasks of lowering sails and securing rig that had come away. In one of the short lulls when the storm wasn't screaming at him, he swore he heard the captain say, "Take her out to deeper water," and he couldn't help feel that he would rather go inshore and find a nice harbour.

On and on, the noise of Kathleen, the roar, the wind and rain, for four hours, they had endured this and just as George began to say, "Enough, no more, PLEASE," the wind stopped, stopped dead as quick as a light being switched off, and so did the rain and all went still. The deck levelled and the sound of storm was replaced by the sound of thousands of drips of water hitting the deck from the sails and rigging. Men came out gingerly from where they were and instantly scanned first, the horizon at all four points, then the sky's, and lastly, the sea and satisfied that, 'that was that', then went about checking for damage as if nothing had happened.

George stepped out from under the poop deck and slowly turned to take in the whole scene, and stopped as Philippo and the captain came into view. They were both stood on the poop deck at the helm. If it were possible for two people to be more wet from head to toe, he knew not how. George climbed the steps and walked to Philippo as the captain passed. "All good, George," the captain said.

"Yes, Captain," George said.

George stood by Philippo and asked if that had been a bad storm, and Philippo replied, "No, it was a good storm," and George was all the more confused as the remaining cloud parted and the sun broke out. In years to come, Philippo would say that this storm had indeed been memorable and not a bad first storm for George, what was certain, it wouldn't be his last.

The rest of the run into Santander was without incident, and after Kathleen had a thorough inspection and given the all clear, it was decided to continue to run on and they got under way again. George scoured the ship for Blue, and eventually, came across him curled up on a pile of canvas below and seemed oblivious and fine. At the point of La Coruna, they heaved to port and sailed down the coast. The captain now changed into dry clothing as had half the crew, turned his attention to the shore through his telescope and completely ignored the horizon which made George uncomfortable. The ship was adorned with wet clothing drying in the sun, something that was acceptable at sea but would never do entering port. "We weren't a Chinese junk," said Jacob.

The captain was looking for landmarks, a church spire or doom, a rock formation, a harbour with a particular entrance, and on each day at the same time, the captain would log day and time and mark on the big chart laid across the table in the state room our position. Santa Maria De Feira welcomed us to Portugal and on we went past Lisbon, any business there would be conducted on our return journey. Day five, we rounded the south-western tip of Portugal and headed east. Past Faro and Huelva hailed Spain, sailed past Cadiz and on to Tarifa with all her fame, we had entered into the Mediterranean and it was clear even to George, these were different waters and climate. George had kicked off his boots and now went about barefoot and this seemed to, in fact, help his balance, not only did he like the feel of Kathleen's wooden deck beneath his feet but he felt a connection to her.

'Gib'

The routine of the past few days was suddenly broken with the captain ordering from the poop to 'break out the anchors' and Kathleen's decks broke into life as anchors were pushed and pulled into place, we were running into Gibraltar.

The bay of Gibraltar. "Let go the anchor," came the cry and the sudden rush of heavy chain and the splash of anchor hitting water announced our arrival.

That afternoon, a row boat came alongside and up the ladder came swiftly four soldiers who took up position at all four corners of the ship baronets fixed. Their commanding office then followed and stepped smartly to the captain, clicked a heel, saluted and said, "Captain Arding, sir, His Majesty's Marines at your command," followed by a smartly dressed man who had struggled with the ladder and arrived on deck in a somewhat disorderly manner which had drawn scorn and mockery from the crew, all be it vailed, he was no seafarer.

As he composed himself, the Marine Officer announced, "His Majesty's consulate, sir, Mister Faringday." Our captain and Faringday shook hands, and after pleasantries exchanged, they went below.

The crew kept their distance from the Marines, traditionally deployed on Royal Navy ships to keep discipline, they had gained a reputation and the nickname, 'boot-necks', from their practice of cutting the top four inches off their high level boots and lacing this backwards on their necks to stop the crew from cutting their throats, such was the relationship.

But George was fascinated with the marines, they were not only smart in appearance but also within themselves, an air of confidents and ability radiated from these man, and for now, they were in total command of this ship.

Sometime later, the captain and Mr Faringday returned to deck. Faringday clutching a large bundle of papers, they said their goodbyes and Faringday clambered down the stairs, and with a barely perceivable order from the Marine Captain, the four marines bound across the deck, formed a close guard as each departed, the last waiting only for their commanding officer as he stepped forward, saluted to our captain turned on his heel and sole and departed himself.

"Up anchor," came the shout with a detectable air of urgency, but urgency not to fight a storm but urgency to lye up and get a run ashore for our next port of call was Malaga.

For Phililppo, Malaga was of special importance, he loved returning to his home port, to see his family, his friends, to eat well and tell stories.

For the captain, Malaga was not just a special port of call but a necessary one too. At a time most needed, to lift the spirits of a man who had just bid farewell to his family and friends, he was talking, of course, of his crew, not himself, he had neither wife nor child, and not a friend to speak of.

'They Got It'

"Drop Anchor," came the shout with a detectable air of excitement, excitement that came in many forms, some loved nothing more than to get ashore and drink, and I mean proper drink, from dusk till dawn, punctuated only by food and return to ship with a disposition that was remarkably and easily remedied with a short slumber. Some seek women, some seek culture and some seek merely to just stay aboard. But for all, it was a very needed short respite to gather 'thy thoughts'.

"George, put on your best attire, we run ashore," said the captain. George pulled from his bag, his good jacket, shirt and trousers he hadn't seen for a while. The captain, Philippo, Jacob and George dropped into one of the row boats and rowed ashore, the captain taking charge of the oars, of course.

There was no black pool, no steam tug, no brick per, just a stony beach that they crunched up to. They disembarked and made their way up through the town until they reached Philippo's house. Philippo's family home was a two-storey building that had a veranda that ran the full length. Philippo's in-tier family now stood on that veranda to welcome him home.

The wildest and most excited whirl of greetings then ensued with Philippo in the midst. First came his mother and father followed by brothers, sisters, aunties, uncles and then the children. George couldn't understand what was being said as it was all in Spanish but he could sense a lot of love and joy, the captain, Jacob and George stepped back for now. Once this whirl had subsided, the attention soon turned to their guests.

The family knew the captain and Jacob very well, and there then followed the traditional handshakes and hugs, a genuine welcome, all conducted in Spanish and George was taken aback at his captain's apparent fluentness in this language. And then there was George, the captain introduced him, Philippo's family swarmed around, and with beaming smiles and warm words of endearment, all to a one began to try and lift George off the ground by the checks of his face. The family retired to the table, two of Philippo's sisters taking George by his hands. Philippo taking pride of place at the head, his father and mother beside him on his right followed by senior members, on his left the captain, Jacob and between the two sisters sat George, and then the rest of the family. Glasses and bottles arrived, and Philippo's father set about charging glasses. George was given a small shot of red wine that was then diluted with water and there then ensued amongst the men at the head of the table more welcomes, salutes and the charging of glasses, once again, whilst they engaged in serious conversation on the topics of the day. The noise of the family was hectic and glorious, and George's head began to spin.

Philippo's mother then stood and patted her hands together, and some members of the family stood and left including the sisters, either side of George, and promptly returned with plates and knives and forks, none of which stopped the conversations around the table. What followed, George could only describe as a never-ending precession of courses, there was soup and fish and meats and pasta, and plates piled high with fresh salad and bread, really good bread. It would seem the two sisters were charged with making sure George got his fill, for every time he finished something, one or both of the sisters would spoon more onto his plate. The only respite was when they would insist on holding his hands, only to then encourage him to have more when they could see he wasn't chewing. This went on for hours, for it was not rushed, people spoke, ate, drank and ate some more. When finally it was decided all had their fill, plates were cleared, although plates and bowls of salad and bread remained, should anyone feel the need of a snack later. George couldn't see how, he was stuffed to the gunnels. However, George did find room for a slice of watermelon and if there was ever a way of finishing off a fabulous meal, this was it.

Philippo's father tapped his glass with a fork, stood and toasted his son. Philippo returned the compliment and extended it to his family, the captain and his crew mates. Philippo's father then toasted the captain and Jacob, and glasses were raised once more by all. Philippo's father then turned his attention to George, and as he raised his glass, the sisters raised George to his feet. Now standing upon the bench, George was cheered by all and he felt a little bashful but also loved.

As the women of the house cleared away the kitchen, the men, deep in conversation, smoked their pipes, and on occasion, clinked a glass. The company was now spread and spalled across the veranda when two of Philippo's family members then appeared with guitars and began to play fast and rhythmically. The family joining in by clapping their hands as someone else sang. One of the sisters and a man began to dance, their heels striking the floorboards, arms flung into the air and skirts were swished and whirled, they did not dance arm in arm but it was no less passionate. George became so taken by and swept along with this scene, he began to clap his hands, and on seeing this, the family cheered, "Bravo, George, bravo." They could see he had 'got it'.

After prolonged farewells, the captain, Jacob and George began their stroll back to the ship. Philippo would spend the night at the family home and re-join them in the morning. As they walked amongst palm trees on a gloriously warm night, George could see and hear families still outside, still eating, children still playing in the street, and yes, he had 'got it'. These people had got it, they ate well, they laughed, they sang, they danced, they loved, they lived.

"Captain," said George.

"Yes. George?"

"Philippo's family must have missed him dearly, how long was he away?"

The captain thought, removed his pipe and said, "About three weeks, but we won't be back this way now for some eight months."

George stopped dead, flung his hands to his face and cupping his cheeks, said, "Eight months? My cheeks won't be able to take it," and the captain and Jacob laughed.

As they approached Kathleen, there came the cry, "Who goes there?"

"The captain," said Jacob. "Come forward and be recognised." They clambered aboard and went directly to their bunks, George did finally fall asleep but only after he had recounted ever wonderful moment of that evening.

The morning came, and with it, the 'routine', the crew was all present and correct, and after breakfast came the order to 'up anchor'. As they sailed out of Malaga, George was joined at the stern by Philippo and the two stood in silence as they watched Malaga fade into the horizon, and George began to understand why a man would feel melancholy on leaving his family and his land.

As they sailed out into the 'The Latin Lake', all sight of land faded away and now from all points of Kathleen, there was water, nothing but water, and it would remain that way for the next couple of days to come. The sea was calm, the sun warm and Kathleen was making good headway on a light breeze. The crew went about their daily routines and watched with an air of contentment.

That night, when supper had finished and George was helping Philippo to clear away, he said, "George, when you have done, you are to report to the captain's quarters." He knew not why, but did as he was told.

Knock, knock. "Enter," came the reply and George walked into the captain's quarters. "Come in, George, and take a seat." George sat at the captain's desk. "How have you been, George?"

"Very well, thank you, Captain, and yourself?"

The captain was somewhat taken aback at someone enquiring as to how he was. "I'm good, George, thank you." "When we first meet, you said you didn't know how to read nor write and that you didn't have a knowledge of numbers, am I correct?"

"Yes, sir."

"Well, George, every man aboard my ship needs to have a knowledge of these things, and so with your permission, I'd like to teach you, what do you say?"

"Yes, sir, I'd like that very much."

The captain produced a leather satchel, some paper and an ink pen. "These are for you." The captain sat by George and proceeded to write in capitals the alphabet, pronouncing the letters as he went. Once he had finished, he wrote again in capitals the word, GEORGE. "Do you recognise that word, George?" He thought it looked familiar but wasn't quite sure, and before George became anxious, the captain said, "It's your name." George could see it now. "Take the pen, George, in whatever hand feels most comfortable, and I want you to look at this line of letters, which are always in this formation. When you find each letter of your name, I want you to write it down and then find the next and so on." George, with nervous excitement, gripped the pen which at first seemed to want to fight him. He looked along the line, and there, there it was, G, and he wrote it down. His writing wasn't as smart as the captain's, but for now, it would do as he wanted to find the next letter and so on. George was reminded of the sack Rosie had written the word London on, and how it had got him here. Soon, there was his name and he had written it, for the first time in his life, he had written his name.

Over the coming weeks and months, when it was convenient, George would join the captain in his quarters and he would learn letters, words, reading, numbers, but also maps of different countries and their whereabouts on the planet, charts and navigation techniques. The captain found George to be a good student, eager, as it wasn't long before George was questioning politely, why this and what of that. For George, he couldn't wait to unlock the next puzzle as it all started to fall into place. He would return at the end of the evening with his satchel now bulging with paperwork, put it in his locker before rolling into his bunk, and with mentally fatigued, fall fast asleep.

"Land ho," came the cry as they approached Sicily. George had never seen such beautiful blue water and so clear, he could see the shadow of Kathleen on the sand banks below them. As George hung over the bow, watching the contrast of the bright blue water and the brilliant white foam being produce by the wake of Kathleen's bow, he became aware of large fish darting in and round the bow, almost making contact but always just in front. George called Jacob over and asked what was this. "Dolphins," said Jacob. "They're our friends," he said and George was in awe.

On to Cyprus and a small respite as the captain delivered paper to the consult of this newly enquired territory, in those days, Britain ruled one fifth of world. Philippo had lowered one of the row boats over the side, and he and George clambered aboard with some fishing gear and rowed out away from the anchored Kathleen and dropped lines into the water. The idea was to catch some fresh fish to supplement the ship's store.

George took charge of the ores in a backward fashion so he could face Philippo, and Philippo made ready the lines. They relaxed back, and after a while, began to bring some fish aboard that would, if nothing else, make good stock or soup. Just then, Philippo's line shot away from him and he said, "George, we have something big," as he began to fight back. The line zipping from one side of the boat to the next, Philippo, not looking, shouted over his shoulder. "George, stop rowing."

"Philippo," George cried and Philippo turned to see George had both ores out of the water. Whatever it was, it was dragging them in circles, whatever it was, it wasn't just big, it was huge. Just as the boat began to bounce and take on water, the line gave with a twang, and all went still and quiet, until the jeers of the crew filled the air. George took up the ores and rowed with all his might back to Kathleen, and they clambered up the rope ladder. The fishing line had been twisted into a spring and the heavy hook completely straightened, and as they stood leaning over the rail, out of breath, George asked Philippo what was that.

Philippo said, "The ocean still holds many secrets, George." Truth is, it was probably a baby reef shark.

George had taken to just wearing a baggy shirt, his work trousers he had cut down to just below the knee and he went everywhere barefoot, such was the weather. Every morning came early and bright, not a cloud in a clear blue sky and it was warm, and it made George feel good. They took a course south towards the north coast of Africa where they would find the entrance to the Suez Canal. Before this channel between the Mediterranean and the Arabian sea was opened in 1869, you would have to fore go the passage around the Cape of Good Hope. This rocky outcrop at the very southern tip of Africa struck fear into all. The ocean here was treacherous and if combined with foul weather, it was indeed with hope that you would make it out the other side alive. So, it was with great relief that this channel was open and not just to save time. The enclosed waters of the Red Sea made it easy and relaxed going, and soon, George, Philippo and the Horton brothers in-gauged in challenges of physical strength. When it came to climbing the rigging, George found he was a natural and swung effortlessly from one to another with shouts of encouragement from the crew below. As they left these calm waters though the Gulf of Aden and out into the Arabian sea, Kathleen's bow began to lift and drop as the waters became a little choppier. George had joined the captain on the poop deck, Philippo at the helm. The captain was preoccupied with something on the horizon, something George couldn't see but the captain would lift his telescope periodically until he looked at George and with nostrils flaring, he said, "Smell that, George?" George couldn't. "Smoke, George. Philippo, take us northwest."

"Aye, aye, Captain."

Pirates

Soon, there came into view on the horizon a curl of dark smoke. "All hands on deck," came the order. Nafe now joined them on the poop deck and there was a noticeable air of seriousness.

"Nathaniel, make ready one of the launches and two of your men, please." Nafe stepped off with purpose. As they approached the sauce of the smoke, George could see a boat but she was low in the water, her mast was still standing but her rigging was gone, and although George could see smoke, it appeared that whatever fire there had been, had fizzled out.

"What is it, Philippo?" asked George.

"A dhow or what's left of her, George."

"What happened to her?" again, George asked.

Philippo, now in-gauged with bringing Kathleen up to, but at a safe distance, from the stricken boat, simple uttered the word, "Pirates."

Dhows are the traditional form of sail boat in these waters, they would be between thirty to fifty feet in length and narrow. They would be used to ferry cargo, usually perishable goods such as fruit and vegetables, from port to port along the coast, so it was unusual to see one this far out, another sign that something wasn't right. Nafe and the Horton brothers climbed aboard the launch, and before rowing out to the sinking boat, the captain shouted down to them to, "Go about, but unless you see any sign of life, do not go aboard her, do you hear?"

"Aye, aye, Capan." The Kathleen jigged about at a safe distance as the crew stood watching with one eye on Nafe, and the other on the horizon in all direction, with a hand gripping tight the handles of their knives. Nafe sat at the bow of the launch as the Horton brothers rowed up to the dhow tentatively. Besides the smoke, there were other tell-tale signs of skulduggery. Nafe could see debris strewn across her deck, there had obviously been a struggle of sorts as there was blood. "Ahoy there," Nafe called out. "Ahoy there," he called again, but there was no response. As they came around her and headed for the bow, Nafe could see her name plate had been wrenched off so if anyone were to come upon her before she sank, she couldn't be identified. Even smaller ships that made short journeys would be expected to arrive at a port in a given time, if they were delayed which often happened, the ports would declare after two or three days that they were overdue, but wouldn't worry unduly. It was only after four or five days that the ship was overdue, that the ports would declare a ship and crew missing, presumed lost and people would begin to look out for her. Removing the name plate and all that could identify a ship would buy the pirates more time to make their escape and difficult to link them to the crime. Nafe was satisfied that there were no survivors and glad he wouldn't have to go aboard a sinking ship, and they rowed back. For the next hour, the Kathleen circled the dying ship like a distraught mother unable to help her child in distress. They would not leave her side until she was gone in order to safeguard other ships in the area. The captain was taking readings from a sextant of her last position, and would hand this information to the authorities at the next port of call. But there was something else that George could sense from the crew, a sense of sorrow, the stricken ship blow funnels of water as the last of the air in her hold escaped, her stern lifted, the water shimmered, and as the last of her slid beneath the water, some of the crew, including the captain, removed their caps and stood in thoughtful silence.

If it was worth carrying than it was worth thieving, and the cargo that Kathleen was about to take on board over the coming months was some of the most prized. Besides the usual luxury items such as precious metals, stones, silks, and spices, there were also other goods that the Kathleen wouldn't be carrying, but were just as prized as booty by the pirates in this area of the south China seas, and that was opium. Whatever took their fancy, it wouldn't take much for a pirate's curiosity, and subsequent interest in you especially, if they could see you were low in the water, with heavy holds of stowage.

Armed and Extremely Dangerous

That night, the watch was doubled and George, after schooling, was given his first watch. George stood between Jacob and Philippo on deck as they explained the duties of the watch, he was to walk the deck and watch the horizon at all four points and if he were to spy another vessel coming towards them, he was to raise the alarm. Jacob looked at Philippo with some uncertainty and said, "He's not even armed, he hasn't even got a knife." Philippo pulled from the rack a belaying pin used to stow coiled rope away neatly and slid this into Georges belt, these pins resemble a club, and on occasion, could be used as one.

Philippo stood back and looked at the skinny three-foot-tall seven-year-old and said, "There, he is now armed and extremely dangerous."

George walked the deck, and despite it being night, the sky was clear and a huge moon meant he could see far into the distance in all directions. As he walked, George would suddenly spin on his heels, simultaneously pulling the pin from his belt, he would then challenge make-believe pirates trying to board the ship, an almighty battle would then ensue with George fighting off and vanquishing the raiders, casting them over the side, saving the ship and all her crew, HURRAH for George the pirate punisher.

"BUMP." George jumped out of his skin, for there at the stern of the ship came a noise. He had been so startled, he had dropped the pin and was now scrambling around on the deck in the gloom trying to retrieve it. From out of the shadows came a large lumbering dark figure moving slowly towards him. George, holding the pin out in front of him as steady as he could, and remembering his duties, he announces in a shaky voice, "Who goes there?"

The captain stopped instantly and said, "It is I, the captain."

116

"Approach one and be recognised," said George, exhaling and the captain snapped to and approached.

"All well, George?"

"Yes, Captain, all's well."

The captain stood a while with George and smoked a pipe whilst they talked. "How long have you been at sea, Captain?"

"I've been at sea, George, since 'Moby-Dick' was a tiddler."

"Captain, do you have a wife and children?"

"No, George, this is no life for a family man, and nor would any sea-fearing man take a wife and children aboard on such a voyage as it was just too perilous to do so. On occasion, you would see a man's family come aboard but only when a ship was safely tethered to a quay." It was a sentiment that would stay with George forever.

Hong Kong

Kathleen manoeuvred into a queue of ships waiting for a pilot to take them quayside. This large bay with a background of mountains standing guard was picturesque, buildings no more than four storeys and spread sporadically. There was a relaxed atmosphere despite the large numbers of dhows and junks going to and throw, some smaller coming up to the ship selling mostly food but also anything you could mention. Hong Kong translated was 'fragrant harbour', and what with so many people in such a relatively small area, George could smell why. They were finally pulled alongside and secured. The captain met with a company man, and soon, cargo began to fill the quay.

The Science of Stowage

From the casual observer, it would be quite obvious that a ship, if filled incorrectly, could lead to quite an uncomfortable voyage, but could also possibly lead to a ship sinking in foul weather. It wasn't just a case of loading a ship with equal quantities on either side to reduce the roll, but it was important as to whether the cargo was stowed heavy forward or aft to increase the comfort and speed of a ship. This knowledge only came from an intimate understanding of the vessel herself, and Jacob, who had sort sanctuary of, and made Kathleen his home knew this 'old girl' with a lot of love and affection and just where to place things to create that 'sweet point'. "Just like a woman, she works best when she a little heavy in da rear," shouted Jacob to the crew as they loaded. The crew all laughed out loud, George laughed along but he knew not why. They took aboard porcelain, destined to adorn the best tables of the of the well-to-do of London, species, silk and cloth. Once all aboard, the Kathleen got under way to Shanghai, her next port of call. From Shanghai and a similar cargo, we stopped at Japan for Lacquer. We then sailed south to Darwin where we picked up precious metals and stones which came aboard in a satchel carried by the captain.

We crossed the Timor Sea and weaved our way around these Islands, we would, on occasion, drop anchor to take on supplies for the ship. The very moment we would do this, Kathleen would be swamped by small local boats selling the very best of local produce, and Philippo would be beside himself with the diversity and freshness of the ingredients. We had a brief stop at Singapore and for some a much needed and eventful run ashore. Back into the Bay of Bengal and the daily routine of ships life. One of the memories of this region that stayed with George was the rains, they were so spontaneous and so heavy, the drops of water would hurt your face and you would have to turn away or seek cover.

Our next stop was Chennai, India, where we took on board silks, spice, wood and ivory. As the weeks and months went by, George busied himself with the day to day tasks of ships duty, watches and his studies. Back through the Red Sea and into the Mediterranean, and on this, the return leg of our voyage, the ports of call would be to procure produce of a more perishable commodity such as fine wines, olives and olive oil. Athens, and the incredible food from the 'meat market', Palermo and the brilliant blue colour of the water. On to Barcelona and we then hugged the Spanish coast all the way south to Malaga where we stopped over for a couple of days, and yes, there was the expected wonderful greeting from Philippo's family. Back through the straights of Gibraltar and a dash across the Bay of Biscay, and as we reached the English Channel, the captain gave Nafe two new name plates to replace those of the Kathleen. They read, 'Geisterfahrer', and we ran up the German maritime flag and sailed past the Russian Navy stood on guard. And so, it was, nine months later to the day we found ourselves back in the port of London.

In years to come, and as tensions between England and Germany heighten, prior to the First World War, questions were asked of the British government about English ships masquerading as German, which the British government hotly denied all knowledge of.

1906, and we were docked in Palermo when we heard a mighty explosion from the east, we later found out that Mount Vesuvius had exploded, devastating Naples. That same year, we were heading for Hong Kong and the captain was pensive, he had noted large numbers of birds flying out to sea and some roosting in the rigging, something wasn't right. As we approached the port of Hong Kong, the very water beneath us started to recede. "Philippo, take us back out, deep and fast," came the shouted orders from the captain. Some miles out, the bow of the Kathleen rose at an angle so steep that it threw all who were on deck to the stern. "Tsunami," came the cry from the captain as we held on. Hong Kong was hit directly, and more than ten thousand people lost their lives.

On leaving the Suez Cannel, we made an impromptu stop at the Port of Alexandria due to foul weather. As George and Jacob leaned over the rail studying the dock, George spied a creature he had never seen before. It was the size of a cow but with a long neck, it sat upon four extremely long legs and had no interest in moving ever fast, and it would seem their owners would, on occasion, have trouble getting them to move at all. Jacob told George, "These animals are called camels and they refer to them as the 'ships of the desert'." George and Jacob ran ashore, Jacob was looking for a chance opportunity to procure some unusual stock that would sell for a good price back in London.

They strolled into a busy Bazaar, people everywhere selling everything from cloth, rugs, and metal wear. The people were dress in long, loose clothing that made sense to George in such close streets and high temperature. Jacob stopped at a forge where the main production was in kitchen utensils, pots and pans, and began to study the quality of those. Attached to the forge was a shop that displayed the finished articles, and George wandered in and over to a glass display cabinet. There laid in the bottom of that cabinet was exactly what George had been looking for, a knife. But this wasn't like the knives the rest of the crew carried which George had always considered to be too broad and heavy, you were more likely to hurt yourself wheeling one of those then an attacker, and George didn't like the way they were carried either, at the front of their belts as if this was a way and means to ward off an assailant.

This knife was more like a dagger and about ten inches long, the handle was of black tightly wound wire with a brass ball at the end. The blade, which was about six inches long, was thin and tapered to a fine point. Jacob negotiated a price for a quantity of kitchen-wear to be delivered to the ship, and with a small amount of begging, Jacob allowed George to have the dagger which he would pay for out of his allowance. In with the price, George got the 'Smith' to put a keen edge along both sides of the blade. The dagger came with a black leather scabbard and George wore this at the small of his back at an angle, so it sat snuggly.

On walking with Philippo back on Kathleen, George felt the dagger being pulled from the scabbard, and on turning, found Philippo examining the dagger intently. "What is this, George, a toothpick?" said Philippo.

"My knife," said George. Philippo began to feel the weight and balance of the dagger and spun it in his hands in a way that led George to realise Philippo wasn't just good at chopping vegetables. Philippo, holding the tip of the blade, brought it up to beside his ear and threw it across the deck, and it embedded itself deep into a beam with a thud. As Philippo hopped over to it to jerk it loose, it continued to make a twanging sound. Philippo again examined the dagger and this time admiringly. George spent the rest of the day fashioning and sewing a loop of leather to the back of the scabbard that would, when the dagger was sheathed, go around one of the 'quillons', the guards that would stop the knife travelling backwards in your hand and cutting you, as a safety device.

1907, and in this year, the Suffragettes stormed the English Parliament demanding the right to vote. Sixty were arrested and Jacob received news of an earthquake in Jamaica that killed more than a thousand people, and the captain organised a 'rum run' to that part of the world.

It was the first time George travelled across the North Atlantic, and although it didn't take long, it was the least desirable of all the voyages because, for a good deal of time, there was nothing but ocean to look at.

We pulled into Kingston Harbour and anchored, despite the misgivings of the captain, Jacob went swiftly ashore to seek out friends and family, he had to. It had been a number of years since Jacob absconded from the plantation and stowed away on Kathleen, and although he had returned on a number of 'rum runs' since, this was the first time he had set foot on the island and thus ran the risk of being recognised. No one else went ashore, there wasn't anything to run ashore for. Port Royal Street was one collapsed building after another, huge pills of rubble filled what once was a busy and bustling thoroughfare, armed guards at every corner. We set about loading not just rum but tobacco too, and on his return, the captain told Jacob to stay below and out of sight. We doubled the watch that night and resumed the loading at first light. By mid-morning, Kathleen's holds were almost full, George was on deck and on watch and under instruction to keep a sharp lookout. Onto the quay came a horse and cart with a man at the reins, two further men followed on horseback, which wasn't out of place nor unusual, but the attention they were giving Kathleen was. George had come accustomed to people standing and admiring the fine fashioning of Kathleen's masts and rigging but these men were not admiring. Before they began to make their way to him, George asked one of the Horton brothers to fetch the captain as he guested at the approaching company. George was joined on deck by the captain and a good number of the crew, Jacob remained out of sight as these men reached the bottom of the gang plank. "Who goes there?" shouted the captain, he already knew what the response was to be.

The man who had been riding on the cart introduced himself as the foreman of a nearby plantation and introduced the two men with him as his 'overseers'. They were all dressed in whites, large brimmed hats, one of the overseers carried a large machete, the other, what could be described as a whip but not the type you would keep a horse in check with, this had more to do with keeping humans in line. "Captain, I have been informed that you have a negro on board," said the foreman as he placed one foot on the gang plank.

"My crew are of no concern of yours, sir, and I would ask of you politely to remove your foot from my gang plank."

"It has everything to do with me, sir, as I suspect this negro to be one that absconded from my plantation some years ago, he is my property and I demand him back." The man, once again, made an attempt to come aboard. The captain opened his long coat and pulled from his belt an 1851 Colt Navy Revolver, and levelled it at the foreman who stopped dead in his tracks. "I will only say this one more time, sir, remove your foot from my gang plank or I shall remove it for you," as the captain said this, he cocked the hammer of the gun back and re-aimed.

"This is not the last of this, sir, I shall return with the port authorities and gain access to your vessel," said the foreman as he stomped off.

"Nathaniel, how close are we to full?" said the captain,.

Nathaniel, unable to take his eyes off of the revolver, said, "We can be under way within the hour, Capan."

"Good see to it would You, please, and tell Jacob to remain below, double the watch and no one is to go ashore."

"Aye, aye, Capan." Nafe turned and then hesitated. "Begging your pardon, Capan, but would you have really done for that man?" asked Nafe.

"Hardly, Nathaniel, this thing's an antique, it's as old as I," said the captain, brandishing the weapon.

We neither saw the foreman nor the port authorities as we finished the load and we were under way within the hour. I was joined by Jacob at the stern as we bade farewell to Jamaica, I glad to see the island disappear on the horizon and I got the impression that Jacob had mixed emotions too.

It was a year or so later on a return leg, we were just coming out of the Arabian Sea and entering the Gulf of Aden when Philippo, who was at the helm, turned to the captain and said, "I believe, Captain, we have a boat following us off port astern."

"Yes, Philippo, she's been there some time, take a more north-easterly course, Philippo, and let's see what she does." Having done this, the ship which was a steam dhow did the same shortly after. "Philippo, take us back onto our original course please," said the captain and Philippo obliged. Shortly after, the steam dhow did exactly the same, the captain and Philippo looked at one another and said at the same time, "Pirates."

"Nathaniel, shorten the main sail, all hands-on deck. Philippo, stay on this course please," and the captain disappeared below.

Nathaniel looked at Philippo and said, "Shorten the main sail? But that will surely slow us, what's the old man thinking, why don't we just out run her?" Nathaniel did as he was told, and sure enough, Kathleen slowed to half her pace. The captain reappeared on the poop deck, hands behind his back and watched as the dhow approached, the crew now on deck also questioned as to what the captain was doing. Just as the wheel house of the steam dhow came into view and you could see clearly the glass windows and figures behind, the captain opened his coat and again pulled from his belt the now-legendary Colt Navy Revolver and levelled it at the dhow. There came an almighty boom as the revolver went off, the front widow of the dhow exploded into a thousand shards, and instantly, its bow dived into the water. Shortly after, the dhow turned swiftly to starboard and made its retreat with heist. Nafe, who had been standing beside the captain, was now on his knees, both hands clasping his ears at the deafening sound the gun had made.

Nafe looked up at Philippo and shouted, "It only bloody works." A huge cheer came from the crew as they waved off the dhow with their knives held high.

As the captain returned below, he was heard mumbling something along the lines of, "Just because its old, doesn't mean it can't work," and "Old man, is it?" That night, over supper came the usual recounts of the day's action from the crew, and toasts came thick and fast to the captain and the Navy Colt.

Back in the Port of London, we heard of yet another disaster concerning a steam ship, with a great loss of life. "Mark my words, George, there has and never will be any good come of these machines, and the sooner they run out of that damned coal the better."

"With all due respect, Captain, I don't think that's likely, sir."

"Why so, George?"

"They have mountains of the black stuff, I've seen it with my own eyes, sir."

In the year of 1908, Henry Ford unveiled his first Model T car, yours for $825, and George couldn't help but think that it won't be the lack of coal that brings about the demise of the machine, but the sheer cost that would kill them off.

The Bodies

Later in this year, we were on our home-ward bound leg, anchored off Palermo, and taking on wine and olive oil, when the British consulate hurriedly came aboard. Once he had left, the captain called all hands-on deck.

"We have received news that a large earthquake has struck Messina not more than two days sail from here. We have been asked to ferry relief supplies to the region, those supplies will arrive quayside within the hour. Jacob, Nathaniel, see to it that these are loaded as quick as you can, as soon as we're able, we make sail, lads."

"Aye, aye, Capan."

The British were received well in this part of the world, particularly sea farers. This region was a great favourite of Lord Nelson and Lady Hamilton, and shortly after his great victory over the French and Spanish armadas off Trafalgar in 1805, there then came the following year a quite extraordinary route of French forces stationed in the region of Calabria, southern Italy, at the village of Maida. A handful of British soldiers marched from Palermo and across the straits of Messina by boat, took on overwhelming French forces and defeated them in spectacular fashion, earning them a special regard in the hearts of the local Italians.

George loved this part of the world, and in particular, the sea of this region for its crystal clarity and a blue so vivid, it would make your eyes water. So, it was with a great shock and disbelief to George as they came about and into the straits of Messina to see the waters so murky and foul of debris, but the most alarming thing to greet George's eyes were the bodies.

Hundreds, if not thousands, of dead people were in the water, lifeless and still. The bow of Kathleen gently nudging these forlorn soul to each side as she went. Men, women, children, and livestock it went on and on for mile after tragic mile, the whole time, fish and birds were having a feeding frenzy, and George felt sickened to the pit of his stomach and had to wear a piece of cloth about his nose and mouth because of the stench. He wished he could have covered his eyes, it was a vision that stayed with him all his life.

Kathleen anchored off the port of Messina and used her two launches around the clock to ferry supplies ashore. We couldn't run the risk of docking in fear of being swamped by desperate people trying to escape the devastation.

We were later informed that eighty thousand men, women and children perished in that disaster.

That year, 1910, and Hailey's Comet brought widespread panic across the world. We buried King Edward VII and a coal mine explosion in England killed nearly four hundred men, and George, momentarily, thought of his father, and this was also the year George got his first pipe, he was thirteen.

The year, 1911, two news-worthy events happened. George V was crowned King of England, and the last horse-drawn vehicle ceased to operate in London, and George recalled the 'black gold' and he wondered, that whatever happened to his good friend, Thomas, with an affectionate smile.

The year, 1912, the Titanic set sail from Queenstown, southern Ireland, on her maiden voyage.

April 14th,1912, she stroke an iceberg and sank in three hours. The Carpathia brought seven hundred and five survivors to New York, all else were feared lost. *The unthinkable befell the unsinkable*, read the headlines and it took two weeks for this tragic news to be known by all upon the planet, despite wireless radio.

In the year of 1913, and we were again in the Port of Malaga, and George was still under the tutelage of the captain. George had grown into a fine and knowledgeable student, able to read and write, carry out complicated arithmetic, plot a course and pinpoint their position. He and the captain would spend many an evening discussing books of the day such at Joseph Conrad's, *The Mirror of the Seas,* and the classic 1851 American novel, *The Whale,* by Herman Melville. George had also grown into a likeable young man, he wasn't tall, in all his years, he never stood any taller than five feet two, but he was quick as lightning on his feet and immensely strong, out-lifting any man aboard, including Philippo. As he stood upon deck, tipping a pail of sea water over his long black curly hair, his powerful physique belied his gentle demeanour.

"George," asked the captain, "when's your birthday?"

"I'm not rightly sure, Captain, I know when I came aboard, I was about six or seven."

"So that would make you about around seventeen," said the captain.

"I guess it would, sir."

"After your duties, George, get into your best rig."

"Why so, Captain?"

"Why, George, why, well, for night, we run ashore, George, for tonight is your birthday," pronounced the captain.

The captain, Jacob, Philippo and George stepped ashore in their best finery, and headed for a family-run restaurant that the captain must have frequented on many occasion as the family greeted us with open arms and genuine smiles. They were shown to the best table and ate heartily, a seven-course meal, washed down with codpiece amounts of good local wine. They moved on to a number of local bars around the port, and as the sun went down, they found themselves at a table watching the sunset and discussing life in general. The captain declaring that, one day, he would drop anchor here, never to move on. Just then, the captain guested to a lady who had been working in the bar. "*Disulpeme, Senora, puede llevar al nino y traerme el hombre por favor?*" (excuse me lady, can you take the boy and bring me the man please?) The lady smiled at George and taking his hand, guested to come with her. "It's OK, George, she wishes to show you something," and they both left.

George returned sometime later, sat and primed the bowl of his new pipe, and set about the serious task of a good smoke, the whole time avoiding eye contact with all present and it was only when after some time the captain forced eye contact and said, "Well?" that George broke into a smile and the rest of the company roared into laughter, which continued for some time between puffs of their pipes.

1914 saw the outbreak of World War I. Clipper ships, such as Kathleen, fared slightly better when it came to avoiding German warships and submarines. Their counter parts, the steam vessels, however, were easily spotted on the horizon because of the smoke they gave off and easily heard from beneath the water because of the noise of their engines. George had seen the recruitment posters and felt he should perhaps do his bit and enquire as to what he needed to do to join up, and it seemed George failed on three accounts. First, he was too young, he needed to be nineteen, second, you had to be five feet three and taller, and at the time, George was barley five one, and third, George had been too honest and because of this, the recruitment staff thanked him and said to come back. Unbeknown to George, Captain Williams had already seen to it that George was exempt from military service because of the work he was already doing through shipping goods necessary for the war effort.

The year of 1915 was spent travelling, mostly at night, without lights and making short and fast runs. All the time came news of yet another British ship being sent to the bottom of some sea, and the huge loss of life and not just on water, it would appear that we were losing men in their thousands in France. Despite George's initial enthusiasm to get involved directly, he now could no longer fathom, no matter how hard he tried to understand what was so valuable above and beyond this human sacrifice. During what was prolonged periods of time spent in London Port, George ventured out to see more of London and it was on one of the excursions he did by chance meet a one Florence Christabel Tricker at the bread and cake shop that the ship's crew frequented.

"Good day to you, my lady, and what brings you here?" said George, who instantly felt stupid as Florence held up some bread in front of her with a beaming smile, eyebrows raised. "Yes, I hear its particularly good here," said George.

"Indeed it is, my house sends me here every day to collect supplies," said Florence.

George removed his cap and said, "Please, excuse me, I'm George Alfred Watkins, at your service, madam."

"And I am Florence Christabel Tricker, very pleased to make your acquaintance, George Alfred Watkins."

"You have a house here in London?"

"No, I work as a maid at the house of a well-to-do family, and you?"

"I have a ship."

"You have a ship?" asked Florence.

"Yes, in the docks, a hundred and ninety eight feet of clipper called the Kathleen, I call her home," George boasted.

"You have obviously done extremely well and so young for a captain," Florence teased.

"Well, I don't wish to bang my own drum, my lady, but praise where praise is due, I am held in high esteem amongst my peers," said George, Florence saw right through George but could sense a good heart and a good nature. They met on a number of occasions and George was struck by her long, black, curly hair, her deep blue eyes that reminded him of the waters around the Islands of Southern Italy. She was small and petite, even beside George, and pretty, very pretty, but despite her size, her most endearing feature was her confidents and attitude, she was savvy and sassy, and George was struck by her.

Florence Christabel Tricker was born on 16th October, 1902, in the small fishing village of Aldeburgh on the Suffolk coast of England. Her parents were Henry and Elizabeth Tricker/King. Florence had four brothers and sisters and possibly one half-sister, they were Dorothy, John, James, Emily and Hollie King/Tricker, and they all lived at 279, the High Street, Aldeburgh, Suffolk. In later years, her brothers, John, James, and sister, Emily, would emigrate to the town of Bennington, Vermont, USA, where they lived, had family and died.

Florence, at the age of fourteen, was sent into service as a maid in a well-to-do house in Central London. The master of the house was the Right Reverend Samuel Reeve and his wife, Elizabeth, they had two children, Emily and Charles.

Florence had travelled down by train to London, having caught a local connection, despite its rural and isolated location, in those days, the region still had good transport connections. Florence, however, despised the small fishing village mentality as she grew up, the same scene, the same people and conversations, and all about the sea and fish. These feelings about this idyllic location, she would come to regret in later life as it would turn out to be a sanctuary of true comfort and safety for which, in years to come, she would only yearn for. She seek challenges, excitement, a place in the big wide world. It was with a little dismay and disappointment when shown her accommodation on the top floor of this large three storey house with a basement, it was somewhat spars compared to the palatial and opulent surroundings of the floors below, but all the house had a distinct lack of a homely feeling.

The Right Reverend Samuel Reeve had spent all his life in the Clergy and had worked his way up, and was now in charge of the local parish. The church was no more than a few streets away and had a congregation of hundreds. The Reverend would always travel by buggy and spend most of the morning away from the house only returning as and when his wife, Elizabeth, and children were visiting the park to perambulate and socialise. He was a slight man in build, and if you didn't know, you would surmise he had suffered or was suffering some form of serious illness. Thin of hair and what was left, he would insist on combing over his bold patch, features were long and thin, and within his parish, he was probably master, however, in his own home, he most certainly wasn't, Elizabeth saw to that.

Florence shared the room on the top floor with Anna, another maid. Anna was from the midlands and had been sent to London to earn money to send home to support her large family of brothers and sisters, she was a few years older than Florence and the two immediately made good friends. The room next door was occupied by the house keeper, Mrs Dawson, who tried where and whenever possible to give direction but it was impossible as the lady of the house, Mrs Reeve, would not in any way, shape nor form, relinquish control of even the smallest nor trifling of tasks, and from the moment they woke to the moment they were dismissed in the evenings, Mrs Reeve was there right behind them directing everything they did.

Elizabeth Reeve had married simple for station in high society and furnished the Reverend with two supposed angelic children to complete a scene of the perfect family. The children were basically good children, but constantly afraid to do or say anything that did not project this image of perfection for their mother. The children would go to school each day until late afternoon, and on some days, would have extra tuition at home for languages and music. Mrs Reeve would hold hi-tea parties three times a week in the afternoon for her extensive circle of snobbish and patronising friends. Each weekend would involve dinner parties which Elizabeth relished in playing the perfect host, something her husband would rather not have had to do, but, of course, he had to do exactly whatever his wife desired, his lack of enthusiasm infuriated her. On these occasions, Mrs Dawson would cook, and Florence and Anna would serve table. The conversation around the table would be of the day and was generally of politics, the war or the struggle of the suffragettes. It was on these occasions that the Revered would try to bring Florence or Anna into the conversation, asking for their opinion about such matters, all skirting about the underlying subject of in-equality. Florence knew he did this amidst these esteemed gatherings purely to further aggravate his wife, and Florence rather he didn't and just allowed them to do their job. He would, of course, eventually stop, but only after his wife had given him a scowl of disapproval, and he would turn inward and drink. It was difficult to know just who here to feel sorry for, if any, perhaps the real victims were the children, bless them.

Florence would rise at five thirty of a morning, put on her work clothes as the first tasks were to set fires in the downstairs' rooms, she would then set about her cleaning routine. By seven, she was ready to wash and change into her maid's uniform, and stood ready to serve the family through their morning. The rest of the day was spent with cleaning chores under the direction of Mrs Reeve and on errands to fetch food or clothes from the seamstress. The house was indeed wonderful, decorated and adorned with the very finest of the then fashion. *If there was ever a people so ill-deserving of such a beautiful home, it was these,* thought Florence.

George was sat on deck killing time before they departed the following morning. He had brought with him his kit bag and in a moment of nostalgia was going through it. He pulled out the train ticket, a single one-way from Mountain Ash, Glamorgan, to Cardiff Central, next was the label his father had tied to his lapel, it read, *George Alfred Watkins 6, C/o 15 Moira Terrace, Cardiff.* The hessian sack that Rosie had written the word London on and there then came the letter that was given to him by Rosie, and he couldn't believe he had forgotten about this for all these years. He gently unfolded the now-limp and somewhat discoloured paper and spread it out across his legs and read.

25th December, 1903
Mr and Mrs George Dunn,
Rose Farm, Farm Lane, Castleton, Cardiff, Wales
My dearest George,

We hope this letter finds you well and in good spirits, and that the long walk to London was not too arduous. Both George and I were sad to see you leave and as I said to you on that day, should you not find London agreeable and not what you were looking for, you would always have a home here with us and the girls.

What I did not explain on the day, George, was we did, in fact, have a son and should he have lived, would have been a little younger than yourself. Having heard your plight and that you were alone and the fact you came to us on Christmas morning, told to me that you were truly God-sent, and I wished I had expressed my feelings toward you more forthrightly at the time, however, my husband, George, felt you should be allowed to stay your course and that you would return to us, should the good Lord deem it so.

Should you get to read this, George, I would like to reiterate to you, once again, my little man, that should you wish to return, do so with the greatest of heist, my dear, for there is a home and family waiting for you here, with open arms.

With great love and affection,
George Rose Ruth Helen

George was taken aback, had never known, he recalled that day well and remembered that as he walked away he had wished he didn't have to go, he wished he could have stayed, and now all these years later, he comes to understand that should he had just turn and looked back at Rosie and George at that very moment, he may have not needed to venture any further, maybe if he hadn't been so frightened to turn in his seat on the train that day perhaps his father would not have sent him away. George was struck with the very sad feeling that, for all theses year, he had not known the love of a family about him.

It was with a new solemn that he stood at the stern of Kathleen and watched London fade that following morning.

The year, 1917, and the United States joined the war and it was generally agreed that the war would be over by Christmas. It was the same year while in the channel, George first heard and then saw his first aeroplane. It did not bellow smoke nor breath fire from its stomach, which George kind of knew it wouldn't, however, what fascinated George was its wings, they were fixed and made no movement.

It was also the year that George met Mary and fell in love. Mary M Prodger was nineteen and was originally from Eastbourne Sussex on the South coast of England. Her father, William, had spent most of his childhood at the Eastbourne Union Workhouse where he learned the profession of gardener. William had been sent to the workhouse as a young child because he had been born without speech or as they referred to it in those days, 'dumb', and thus his family could not cope with him. Mary, as soon as she could, made the move to London for work during the First World War and found employment with the railways as a sewing machinist making upholstery. They had a whirlwind romance, spending every moment they could together and it felt right when George proposed one evening, and soon after, they had a simple ceremony and became man and wife. George rented a single room in a shared house close to the docks and spent most evenings there as opposed to on ship, which despite the ribbing from the crew, no one minded, and in fact, people were pleased to see George happy. However, the inevitable day came when George would have to go back to sea, 'it's what he did', for now. The evening before they departed, Mary told George that she was with child and that, on his return, he was to be a father, George was beside himself with joy. The following morning, and yet again, George experienced another type of goodbye, being waved off by Mary from the docks, the crew making him blush with their jeers.

George had mixed emotions. Sure he was sad to leave his new wife, but the landlady who they rented the room from also lived in the same house and had promised George to look out for Mary, so it wasn't as though she would be all on her own. "And besides, before you know it, I'll be home," he said and it felt good to say 'home'.

This run was somewhat different from previous, there were a number of ports we simply could not enter because, in this year, there was the outbreak and global spread of Spanish Flu. This, in turn, meant we would more often than not stop at ports we hadn't frequented before and a change in some types of cargo we would take on board. We had a hold full of exotic woods from India, and yards of cloth and silk as well as barrels of cinnamon. This run was also different in that George couldn't wait for and wished for the half-way point as he knew they were on their way home. Of course, there was no way he could let Mary know about their position, they had no ship to shore wireless, although it was available, it was expensive to fit and as the captain said, "We've not had the need before and we do not need it now." As they got closer to England, the more excited George became and the more people would congratulate him on the prospect of being a father and what did he want, a boy or a girl, he said he didn't mind, but deep down, he wanted a boy.

The morning of their arrival and George was up early in the hope that if he got his duties over and done early, he could run ashore that much sooner. By the time Kathleen was being pulled alongside, George had not only completed his duties but had washed and was changed into his good rig. "Sorry, lads, but we need to get this cargo ashore before we get leave, which means we'll be at it all day," shouted the captain. George's shoulders visibly went down as he stood on deck surrounded by the rest of the crew in total silent. Just then, a mighty roar of laughter rose up from everyone aboard which made everyone on the dock stop and look to see what was happening, everyone was slapping George on the back.

"You mean we don't have to stay and unload, Captain?" said George.

"Oh, yes, George, this slovenly lot will be here till late, but every man to a one has asked for you to be relieved of this duty so you can run ashore now."

George was overcome with emotion and was told to, "Get ashore now, you silly sod, before we change our minds."

George grabbed the silk shawl he had bought in Ceylon for Mary, he stopped at the market and purchased bags full of fresh fruit and vegetables, and some prime cuts of meat. He had asked Philippo to give him some tips on cooking, which he was all too glad to oblige, and George was going to cook for his wife tonight, his last purchase, a bunch of flowers, and he was done.

George turned into the street and stopped outside the house. He removed his cap, straightened his hair and knocked on the front door. He wouldn't walk straight in, it didn't seem right as he hadn't stayed there that long before he had gone back to sea. The landlady, as expected, answered the door as George beamed, the landlady gasped, hands to her cheeks, eyes wide and said, "Oh, George."

The landlady's husband asked George in and as he stood with his flowers in hand, the man said, "Mary and child died in birth, George, we're so sorry."

George was rocked to his core and all he could ask was, "Where are they?"

"They're buried at St Augustine's," the husband said, and George left.

George ran from one group of headstones to the next. It was raining and he didn't care, he stopped as he came across a fresh grave, one small posy of flowers laid upon it and he knew. As George approached, he read, MARY WATKINS and SON, GEORGE. He collapsed, fell and laid alongside the grave, one arm around the pile of soil as if it were around Mary's waist and there he stayed. Night turned into day and day to night, the only subsidence George had was the occasional swig from a bottle of whiskey. By day-three, George was soaked to the skin and shivering uncontrollable, he had become delirious and began to hallucinate, people kept coming to him. Mary, his son, he never meet his mother. He had been so cold but now even that had subsided away and a small smile came across his face as he became numb. He could hear his heart, da dum, da dum, it became slower and slower, the light faded and became a small speak in the distance, he became weightless and lifeless, and he felt his body lift skyward, his limbs out-stretched and then the darkness closed in and there was nothing.

When George had not returned to ship on a given time and day, Captain Williams had gone in search. He had sensed something wasn't right, it was unlike George and out of character. The captain had found the lodgings, and was informed of the tragic events and given directions to the cemetery where he found George huddled against Mary's grave, soaked through and barely alive. The captain, wasting no time, grabbed George by his jacket, lifted him skyward and flung him across his shoulders and made heist back to the ship. As the captain reached the gang plank, he called out for help. Philippo, Jacob and Nathaniel all appeared, and the captain began to give orders, "Light the fire in my quarters, Philippo, bring me all the hot water bottles you have and prepare some hot broth, Jacob, help me with him."

They got George to the captain's quarters, and stripped him out of his soaking cold clothes and laid him in the captain's bed. Stone hot water bottles were laid about him and the captain removed his boots and jacket, and climbed in beside George and held him close to try and transfer some of his body heat to his. It was four hours before George's outer extremities regained some form of heat but George was still unconscious and remained so for three days. The captain sat for night and day, and watched over him, only relieved on occasion by Jacob, Philippo or Nathaniel. Finally, on day-four, George came to, and on opening his eyes, wondered if he was in heaven as he didn't recognise his surroundings. "There you are, George, good to have you back, my boy, you've had us all worried." The captain stood and went to the door, and shouted for Philippo who came quickly. Philippo's face went from solemn to a smile when he saw that George's eyes were open.

"We'll have that broth now please, Philippo."

"Aye, aye, Captain," said Philippo, as he nodded at George. It was a week before George was fully on his feet and back at his duties.

During that week, George and the captain sat for many an hour and talked. George trying to make sense of his loss, at one point, expressing that he would rather be dead himself, to which the captain's response was to say, "Nonsense, George, there has been two sad and unfortunate deaths, that of your wife and your son, what possible good would it do, should you die because of this? All would be surely lost, for within you now, their memory lives on and will continue to do so, be thankful, my son, for the time you had." This did indeed sooth some of the pain.

Dark Times

George went inward, he was not himself, no longer the laughing joking young man he had been. He wasn't unpleasant, and of course, never rude but his spark had died and all about him could sense it. The spark had been replaced with a seriousness, a coldness if you like and a slight intolerance.

They had pulled into Hong Kong harbour, it was night, and George had finished his duties and made his way ashore alone. George's first stop was at a store to pick up a bottle of whiskey which he slipped into his great coat pocket. He had begun to drink, not that he didn't drink before, he did, but that was for enjoyment, now he seemed to drink just to forget, to numb his feelings. On leaving the store, he spotted the small gang of locals stood at the street corner. There were three of them, and although they made an attempt to pretend they were not interested in him, George knew exactly why they were there and what their intention was, and George made a show of counting his change before he placed it into his trouser pocket. George walked deliberately slowly and took a path that no person with their safety in mind would ever take. Sure enough, the three Hong Kong locals appeared in front of George, and without a word, the three pulled knives and one pointed to the money in his pocket, and George just stood and looked at them. They, in turn, became agitated at George's lack of acknowledgment and weary at the unusual lack of fear from George. George took the bottle from his pocket, and took a long hard pull of the whiskey and replaced the cork. As he went to place the bottle back, the first man, having lost his patience, lunged for George, George hit the man hard between his lower jaw and the bridge of his nose with the whiskey bottle, the man was upended, the impact of the blow had forced the man's face to concave, all shape of his nose was gone and he had lost most of his front teeth. Also suffering laceration as the bottle gave way and broke, he crumpled into the cobbles and instantly went motionless. Holding the remains of the bottle, George now slid his dagger from the small of his back and now stood arms out to his side, his head tilted to one side, he smiled a cruel and careless smile at the remaining two attackers.

The two remaining attackers had gone from bravado to visibly shaken to their core, for there before them stood death in all its personification. They could sense George had no care for his own safety, they could smell death, their own, and they knew if they did not leave, then this day would be their last upon this planet and so they did, leaving their companion on the ground. As the echo of their feet could be heard running away, George looked at the broken bottle and said, "What a terrible waste of perfectly good whiskey, shame."

The year, 1919, World War I came to an end. Kathleen was back in London and George found himself dockside, watching the hustle and bustle from a tavern but not really caring too much, when just then he recognised a movement, a shape, a figure and his eyes began to follow. Was it or wasn't it, he couldn't tell there were too many people in the way. George jumped up, throwing some coins on the table for the ale he'd been drinking and began darting though the crowds. As he approached the figure, he couldn't help but wonder why no prime-starched maid's uniform, why the dark grey dirty clothes of the workhouse? "Florence," he called, the figure didn't stop. "Florence, is that you?" The figure stopped but did not turn, George walked around her, she looked at the ground and would not make eye contact. "Florence, is that you?" He lifted her face by her chin, and yes, it was Florence but she was pale and thin, a shadow of what he remembered. "Florence, what has happened?" With this, Florence collapsed into his arms and sobbed uncontrollably. George, with his arms around her, could now feel just how little Florence had eaten in the last few weeks. George half-carried and half-walked Florence to a local kitchen, they sat and George ordered a bowl of hot salt beef stew, bread for Florence and a tankard of ale for himself. George made ready his pipe as he watched Florence eat with both hands without purse nor taking a breath. Finally, she had wiped the bowl clean with the last of the bread, and sat back and breathed as if out of breath. George finally said, "What has happened, Florence?"

She looked at her hands and realised that there was no point in saying nothing, nor trying to make light of the situation, for George had been the only friendly face she had seen in weeks. "I'm in the workhouse and pregnant, George." George took the pipe from his mouth and gave a look of disbelief and one that demanded an explanation.

"It all began one afternoon when I was alone in the house. Mrs Reeve was out with the children and both, Mrs Dawson and Anna, were on earns. I had returned to my room to change from my work clothes as the duties of the day were done and was changing into my maid's outfit for the return of the family. There came a knock at the door which then opened immediately and in walked the Reverend Reeve. I was caught in just my undergarments, I lifted my work's dress to cover myself. The Reverend said, 'Ah, Florence, how are we?' as he walked to the window.

"'Fine, sir.'

"Sensing my discomfort, he said, 'Don't be frightened, my child, I will not hurt you. I gather, Florence, you are from Alderbough in Suffolk, aren't you?'

"'Yes, sir, I am.'

"'Yes, I know the parish well and the Reverend there, we are on good terms. Your parents, Florence, are they God-fearing people?'

"'Yes, sir, they always attend church on a Sunday, sir.'

"'Good, Florence, good to know people serve the church, just as you serve me. Now lower that dress and remove your undergarments and show me what the good lord has given you.'

"'I shall not,' I said with disbelief and anger.'

"'Oh you shall, Florence, for where will you go, should you be dismissed from this house in disgrace, home! I think not when your family have been forced from the church, and in such a small community to, now remove your clothes.' I wept, dropped my dress and removed my undergarments and stood naked. 'Now turn around for me.' I did, and on doing, so the Reverend strode past with the words, 'Good girl, now get dressed,' and he was gone."

Over the coming weeks, the visits from the Revered became more frequent and the sexual demands more explicit, and always with the threats toward her family, until inevitably, one afternoon, the Reverend raped Florence.

Some weeks later and Anna came downstairs to begin her duties to be met by Mrs Reeve. "Where is Florence?"

"Beg your pardon, ma'am, but Florence is not feeling herself at this moment, I'm not sure she is fit for duty." Mrs Reeve pushed past Anna and raced up the stairs and barged into Florence's room to find her throwing up into her chamber pot. There shortly came a visit from the doctor and Anna couldn't help feel that Mrs Reeve was so considerate, little did she now.

After the doctor had examined Florence whilst Mrs Reeve was present, he turned to her and said in a lowered voice, "I can confirm she is pregnant."

"How far gone is she?" said Mrs Reeve.

"About eight weeks, I would say."

"Thank you, Doctor, that will be all."

The doctor left and moments later, in the doorway, appeared the Reverend. "What has happened, Elizabeth?"

"As if you didn't know," hissed Elizabeth. "I am sick and tired of clearing up yet another of your little indiscretions, Samuel, get out of my sight," she shouted. Elizabeth now turned to Florence and calmly said, "Shortly, someone will arrive for you, I want you to gather your belongings and be ready."

"Where am I to go?" said Florence.

"To the workhouse, Florence," and she leaned in and said, "I'm a patron of this workhouse, utter a single word of this, Florence, and I shall reach out and make your life extremely difficult, do you hear?" Florence nodded.

Although the workhouses were run by charitable organisations such as the church and supposed to be financed by them, in reality and behind the scenes, they were run by the 'gangs' that took care of discipline and took advantage of this endless sauce of human misery to benefit them in the pursuit of anything criminal, and any and all proceeds were divided between themselves and the 'governors'.

George was stunned, he could not believe what had happened to Florence and at the hands of a supposed man of the cloth too. Florence was now sat, sobbing. George relit his pipe and said, "OK, Florence, this is what I want you to do."

George returned to ship and asked Captain Williams if they could speak, the conversation went long into the night. The captain completely understood George's thinking, perhaps there was another way of life beside that of life on an ocean wave. In recent months, the captain had seen an increase of steamers in the ports and as much as he didn't wish to acknowledge the fact in public, these machine were becoming reliable and thus the bulk of new contracts were going their way. The captain had already begun to try and formulate what was to become of Kathleen, and it was with some relief that George had pre-empted this and had decided to make the break. The following morning, George had packed his kit and was stood on deck, he said goodbye to Jacob and Nathaniel, Philippo gave him his family's address in Malaga to write to and George gave Philippo his dagger, and all embraced. George made his way to the poop deck where the captain was stood. "Well, I guess this is it," said George.

"I guess so," said the captain. "George, it's been some time since you came aboard, and during that time, I have taken you under my wing, you are the closest I have come to having a son. If you had stayed, I guess, one day, you would have taken over the Kathleen, but at present, I am having my doubt for the future of Kathleen myself. I wish you all the very best for the future, George, it's been a pleasure," and the two men shook hands which led to an embraces.

In years to come, George did indeed write letters which he sent to Philippo's family address, and to his surprise, back came a response. The captain, not long after George left, sailed Kathleen one last time to Malaga where he tied up quayside and then set about refitting Kathleen and she became a floating restaurant with Philippo in charge. The captain and Jacob spent their days fishing to supplement the kitchen and it soon became a roaring success. There were, of course, the invites to George and Florence to visit Spain but they never did, how could he, he didn't possess a passport. Nathaniel stayed in London and became a prominent figure in the unions representing the Dockers.

Florence, that morning, went about her usual routine that she had become accustomed to in the workhouse. She helped the younger women and children wash and get dressed before breakfast, the young would then be sent to do hard work of one sort or another, and for long hours, some of the older girls would be pushed into prostitution. Florence was, for now, exempt from all such work because of her condition, but she knew as soon as she had her baby, she would be taken advantage of. Florence, not wanting to attract attention nor raise suspicion, calmly helped clear away the breakfast dishes and continued with her cleaning tasks around the house, the whole time trying desperately to hide her fear of being caught. She dashed between cleaning jobs in the dormitories to fill a pillow case with all she possessed, a lot of her clothes had been taken from her when she arrived, as they were deemed too good for the workhouse and would create resentment amongst the others, in truth, the clothes would have been sold on.

By mid-morning, most of the occupants of the house were out working or on errands. Florence peeped out of the upstairs back window overlooking the yard with fingers crossed. "Please be there, George, please." Sure enough, there he was, leaned against a wall in the alley, smoking his pipe. Florence gave a little wave, and George looked up and down the alley and gave the thumbs up. Florence slid the sash window up as quietly as she could, she then took her bundle of clothes and dropped them to George who had darted into the yard and on catching them went directly to the street to wait for her. Florence threw a shawl around her shoulders, took a deep breath and began to walk down to the front door of the house, she physically had to slow her pace as she drew closer.

With one hand on the door handle, there came from behind her the voice of one of the members of female staff, "And where do you think you're going, Florence?"

Florence paused, she could feel herself trembling but she had to compose herself. Florence turned, and with a nice smile and an air of confidence, she pulled from her piny pocket a piece of paper she had placed there that morning and holding it out toward the woman, said, "The mistress has sent me on some errands, ma'am." In fact, the paper was blank and Florence was taking a huge gamble.

"Well then, don't dilly dally, be off with you, and make sure you're back to serve food at lunch, do you hear?"

"Yes, ma'am." Florence swiftly turned and she was out the door, she couldn't believe it, she was free.

On seeing her leave the house, George began to walk and Florence, as instructed, followed some twenty feet behind until they were a few streets away and George nodded for her to join him. Florence hugged George as she came close. "We did it, George."

"Not quite, Florence."

"Why so?"

"The gang," said George.

"They've seen us," said Florence.

"They saw as soon as you threw your clothes from the window and have followed us ever since."

"Oh no, George, what can we do?"

"Leave that to me, my dear." George deliberately turned into an alley, and sure enough, the gang took advantage, they took the bait.

"Well, well, well what do we have here then." There were three of them, the man in the middle was the leader, the two either side were carrying cudgels. "Florence, isn't it?" Florence didn't answer. "I'm disappointed, Florence, wanting to leave us so soon, you haven't even begun to pay us back for our kindness and charity, something I was personally looking forward to, my lovely."

George stepped forward and said, "Gentlemen, we seek no trouble, we simply wish to be on our way."

Jerking forward, the leader snarled, "And what's this got to do with you?" George recognised this man, something about his eyes and George suddenly recalled the very day he stepped onto the dock and a lad had flipped his cap off. This lad had turned into a man and that man now stood before him.

George turned and looked at Florence. "This lady, gentlemen, is to be my wife and the child she carries is to be my son." Florence's chest swelled as she looked proudly at George, at her man.

George raised his hand slowly to the brim of his cap and said, "We bid you good day, gentlemen."

The men went visible taut with tension and from over George's shoulder came these words from Florence, "Get 'em, George."

George flung his cap into the face of the man on the right, at the same time. he hit the leader square in the face with a straight sharp left and he went backwards. George then turned to the man on the left and hit him with a right cross, and the way in which he crumpled and went down, told George this was no fighting man. He turned back to the man he had flung the cap at, who at this point, had raised the cudgel he was carrying. George ducked under and hit him with a left upper cut into his ribs, the man's arm immediately came down with the pain, and George followed up with a left hook to the chin, followed by a right cross and he was done. The leader, at this point, had scrambled to his feet and still half-bent over when George nonchalantly kneed him to his temple and he was instantly knocked out, crashing face first into the gutter, on seeing this, the other two lost their passion for the fight, and ran.

George graded their belongings and said calmly, "OK, let's be off." Florence looked on with bewilderment and awe at what just happened. They walked for a further few streets just to get out of the area and stopped.

Florence said, "George, where are we to go?"

"Florence, you said you were from the Suffolk coast."

"Yes, but I can't go back there."

"Why not?"

"Because half my family have emigrated to America, and what if the Reverend and his wife decide to pursue the rest of my family through the church, I couldn't take the embarrassment, George."

"OK then, Norwich it is."

"Norwich," said Florence.

"Yes, I've heard it's a fine city," said George.

"And how are we to get there, George?" said Florence.

George looked skyward and said, "It's fine weather, Florence, we'll walk," and he stepped off.

"But, George…" came the cry from Florence. And so, it was that, in 1920, the first days of prohibition began in the United States, an earthquake in China kills more than two hundred thousand people, and George and Florence began their walk to a new life in the fine city of Norwich, Norfolk.

Another Long Walk

It didn't take long for the city's industrial sprawl to give way to countryside and open fields. Despite having to walk, Florence hadn't felt so happy and safe since she left her home in Suffolk. The traffic on the road consisted of heavily leaden vehicles heading into London and partially empty coming out so it wasn't difficult to get offers of rides from passing drivers, particularly as Florence found a new talent of playing the part of the pregnant lady. This time of the year brought the 'turkey droves', and on a number of occasions, they found themselves swamped by hundreds, if not thousands, of turkeys on the road, which Florence could deal with if sat at the back of a cart, but soon, became flustered if these birds were flapping around her ankles, much to the amusement of George who would end up having to pick Florence up in his arms and hold her until the birds had passed. These drives were sessional, and began in August and went on all the way up until Christmas. Most of the flocks would originate in Norfolk and the journey would begin with the birds having their feet coated in tar as they walked through pits of it, this was to protect them from the road surface as they walked along.

The entire reason George had decided to walk was born out of finance, he had received a good amount of pay from the captain but this would soon be eaten up if they were not careful. They had to arrive with as much money they could in Norwich to secure accommodation. They needed first and foremost to get a roof over their heads, and although George was sure he would find work and quickly, you just never knew. Despite this, George was not about to ask the mother of his unborn son to sleep in barns and under trees looking at the stars, so they would pace their journey so that, at the end of each day, they would arrive at a market town where they would find accommodation for the night and a chance to wash and eat some hot food. The journey enabled both George and Florence to really get to know one another. As they strolled country lanes, George for the first time told Florence of his past, his mother, his father and the seven brothers and sisters he was forced to leave behind, including his twin sister, Sarah Annie. Florence was disgusted and appalled in the treatment of George by his family. George, having had to cope with this for many a year, simply shrugged this off as, "Families had to do what they had to do back then." It was without doubt that, on this journey, George and Florence bonded. Florence told George that she had never realised just how good an upbringing she had on the Suffolk coast and the last few years in London had proved this to her.

As they went from Suffolk to Norfolk, 'Nelson's county', there was a noticeable difference in the lay of the land, where George thought Suffolk was flat, Norfolk exceled herself. George thought, *If it wasn't for hedge rows and trees, you could probably see all the way to the North Sea.* It was no wonder this was the bread bowl of England with field after field stretched out before them for miles.

Norwich, a Fine City

Norwich was an ancient city, with one of the largest population for many a year, even compared to London. Some of the first recordings go back to the rebellion of AD 60 when Boudica, the leader of the British Celtic Iceni Tribe, led an uprising against the occupying forces of the Romans Empire, just south of Norwich, and also the sacking of the city by Vikings hordes. It played a big part in the early history of England, a city that played a powerful role, in industry, politic and agriculture. The city also gained a reputation for being somewhat bohemian, in that it would welcome artists, from all over Europe and became a centre of literal excellence. It also became synonymous with rebelling against the powers of the day, the most famous of which was Kett's uprising of 1549 which was quelled by the then government hiring Germany mercenary's to put Kett and his men down.

Norwich of 1920 was a thriving, modern city, despite being somewhat off the beaten track, became a major industry in wool and one of the largest suppliers of cloth, even rivalling the massive mills of the north. The city was also known for its shoe manufacturing and there were several rival factories all producing high-quality product, and of course, there were several breweries, the city could boast that there was a pub for every day of the year, and some. All of these industries took advantage of the road and canals systems, and also the links to the coast and Europe via the coastal port of Great Yarmouth, so there were good lines of communication and transportation. The first recorded shops in England opened in an area of the city called 'back of the Inn', and many rich merchants built luxury homes in Elm Hill, the ground floor of a brick construction and upper floors built with timber, such was the fear of fire bombing. Despite the city having an electric tram system since 1900, a large part of the inner city's commercial transportation was still carried out by horse and cart, and George thought with a chuckle, he could always go back to being a shoveller. Norwich was indeed a fine city that was going places and the general vibe was exciting.

On arriving in Norwich, they found themselves in an area of the city centre known as Burr Street, this street was synonymous and notorious with crime, violence and prostitution, however, the rent was cheap. They rented two rooms in a shared house, and shared the toilet which was outside and a small kitchen. The rooms had no furniture, but that was the least of their worries as George needed to find work and as soon as possible.

George spent the days walking the city and enquiring at different companies about work, many of which turned him away as they simply had nothing to offer. He was eventually given work at Moran's Brewery. George's knowledge of barrels and stowage would come in very handy, particularly when it came to handling and loading barges. George was asked to start Monday and settled in right away. Within the week and after receiving his first wage, he asked to borrow one of the company's large barrows to collect some furniture from the market, and soon, Florence began to make her nest. Norwich market had been a feature of the city for as long as the city itself, nestled at the foot of the castle it was, and still is one of the largest undercover markets in Europe, a place you could find anything.

Family

George was sat in the other room, pensive, on edge. He had been woken early that morning by Florence who had clearly gone into labour. George had informed the midwife on his way to let the brewery know he wouldn't be in because of the circumstance, they in turn told him to take whatever time he needed. After some hours, the midwife appeared and said, "Both mum and child are fine," and George beamed.

"May I go in?" said George.

"Yes, of course. And by the way, Mr Watkins, You have a bonny daughter."

"Daughter," said George, clearly expecting a son. George joined Florence and child on the bed, and put his arms around both, leaned in and kissed Florence on the lips. "Well done, darling, how are you feeling?"

"Tired," said Florence, "But OK."

"And who is this?" said George, smiling at the little bundle in her arms.

"George, I like you to meet your daughter, Coney."

George took the baby in his arms, and held her close and kissed her on her forehead. "Hello, Coney, welcome to this world."

George, Florence and Coney had been at Burr Street for a year now, and even the prostitutes had stop propositioning George on his way home from work and now greeted him with an "Evening, George, how's the family?" as he passed.

There was something about living in a notorious area, everyone looked out for each other, you were actually less likely to fall victim to crime because of it.

In the year, 1922, and the tomb of an Egyptian King was unearthed in Egypt and Florence gave birth to their second child.

"Have you brought me a son, Florence?" beamed George as he joined mother and child.

"Meet daughter number two, George," and George laughed. In those early days, George, at the weekends, would have to walk to the outskirts of Norwich and surrounding fields where he would forge for seasonal vegetables to just make ends meet.

In the year, 1923, Florence fell pregnant and because the rooms on Burr Street were now deemed to be over-crowded or would soon become, the council gave the Watkins Family a four-bed semi-detached house in Norwich. 104 Beverly Road was for Florence a veritable palace, there were four large bedrooms upstairs off a landing, a front room that looked out onto and small front garden, and Beverley Road beyond. There was a middle room that was generally used as a dining room but sometimes would double up as another bedroom, a kitchen that had a gas stove and oven, built-in cupboards, a pantry and running water. The bathroom was just beyond, and it had a sink and a full-length cast-iron bath that was so big that, in later years, Florence was able to bathe all the younger children in one go, this too had mains running water. The toilet was in the yard along with the coal shed, and all four bedrooms, front room and dining room had fireplaces. Florence was beside herself, and felt so lucky to have been given such a beautiful house and straight away set about making a home for her expanding brood. George, yet again, borrowed a barrow from work and that weekend ferried bits of furniture from different parts of Norwich. George was himself over-joyed, for 104 Beverly Road had one other luxury, that of a large back garden. George wasted no time and set about turning over the soil in the entire back garden, that had been originally laid to grass, and soon thereafter, George began to produce good quantities of potatoes, carrots, onions, coli and beans, which Florence would turn into the most marvellous of meals. But George didn't stop there, he commandeered some wooden packing boxes and broke them down, and with some wire, constructed a coop, and once the chickens had settled in, began to bring them fresh eggs, so many in fact that Florence was able to bake and from then on, there was always cake for the weekend.

In 1924, Florence gave birth in their new home. "Well, Florence, another girl?" said George.

"No, George, congratulations, you have a son."

George, wide-eyed and smiling from ear to ear picked up, his new-born son and said, "Welcome to the world, George." It came as no surprise to Florence that George gave his first son his name just as his father had done with him, little did she know it was, in fact, George's mother, Dinah, who had named him.

In 1925, Florence was again pregnant but not expecting any day soon and thus had no concerns as she started her day.

"George," shouted out the foreman as he stepped onto the warehouse floor.

"Here," said George.

"A neighbour of yours, George, has just come into the office to say Florence and baby have taken ill, and are now on their way to the hospital." George panicked and went to run. "George, get Harry to take you in the truck," shouted the foreman.

George reached the hospital to find Florence in bed in a ward and she looked pale and drained. The doctors, realising that the baby was in trouble, induced an early birth. "Mr Watkins," said a doctor.

"Yes?"

"What blood group are you?"

"I'm not rightly sure," said George.

"Come with me, we'll do some tests." George was a match. "If your son is to stand any chance of surviving, we need to carry out a blood transfusion right away, Mr Watkins."

"Son?" said George, momentarily distracted. "Yes, yes take what you need," said George. There then followed hours and hours of waiting, George stayed by Florence's bedside the whole time.

The following morning, as Florence managed to eat something, George was called away. "Mr Watkins, we did everything we possibly could, but I'm afraid your son was just too premature, I'm really sorry. Can I leave you to inform your wife?"

"Yes, I shall and thank you, Doctor." As the doctor turned to go, George asked, "Doctor, can I see him?"

"Yes, I'll ask the matron to make arrangements."

"Thank you," George said again.

"He didn't make it, did he, George?" said Florence.

"No, sweetheart, he didn't." Florence rolled over and cried herself to sleep, and after a while, George left her to rest. Laid on a gurney with a pillow case across him was George's son, he was tiny, even for a premature baby, but perfectly formed, he had a full head of black hair. George took his hand between finger and thumb and whispered, "I'm so sorry, boy."

Florence insisted on signing the birth certificate on which she wrote the name, Russel Watkins.

In the year of 1927, the last Model T Ford car came off the production line, and Mr Ford had managed to make and sell fifteen million of them worldwide. The same year, Charles Lindbergh flew, one of those machines from New York to Paris. It would seem the machines had not just arrived, they were here to stay. But not for George, he never took a driving test, not that you had to in those days, and he never would, he had a distinct lack of trust for machine, and in all his life, he never once drove a car and instead he placed his trust in a good old-fashioned and reliable bicycle to get him to where he needed to be. It was in this year that their third daughter was born and Florence first observed something peculiar about her first child, Coney, without prompt, the child had developed a love of all things religious.

In the year of 1929, 'the Great Depression' began to take grip in America. Televisions became a thing, of course, George would never have one in the house even if he had been able to afford one as they were a lot of money and every penny was spoken for in the Watkins' household. Some gangsters were shot in Chicago on valentine's day, and it was on this day, their next child was born. "Another girl," said George sarcastically.

"No, George, you have another son, and he is to be called Russel," said Florence.

In the year 1930, the game of football held its very first world cup and George scored a goal of his own, for nine months later came their next child. "Girl?" said George.

"No, husband," said Florence, and so, Bernard came into the world, a world that began to see the British Empire begin to crumble.

1932 came and went without much to report, and there came no children for Florence and George for once.

The year, 1933, and people were concerned with a man by the name of Hitler who had just formed a new government in Germany with overwhelming support from his people. George couldn't really see what all the fuss was about, he seemed all right, just a bit excitable. It was also the year that Florence was yet again heavy with child when she walked into the coal shed to grab a pail of coal, and was frightened by a mouse and miscarried.

In the year 1934, and their next child was born. "Boy?" said George.

"No sorry, George, girl."

This was the year the Atomic bomb was designed, and George couldn't fathom the thinking behind creating a weapon that could destroy the very planet we live on. "As if there was somewhere else we could go." The trams in Norwich ceased to be and were replaced by busses, and in America, in 1935, a child was born to a family and they named him Elvis.

In the year 1936, and Edward VIII abdicated and the Spanish Civil War broke out, and George thought of Philippo and his family. Back at Beverley Road and Russel fell ill, he had a fever and a cough, and spend the next few days laid on the settee in the front room being cared for by Florence who did all she could to make him comfortable during this heavy cold. George had stopped at the Grove Pub for a pint, something he did most evenings after work before heading home for his tea. As he turned the corner, there in the street was an ambulance and a police car, an officer standing outside his house talking to neighbours. George dropped his lunch pail and ran past the police officer who tried to stop him, up the path to be meet by Florence. "It's Russel, George, he's dead," said Florence, eyes filled with tears. George, visibly and emotionally, collapsed. Russel, unbeknown to all, had contracted Diphtheria, and despite being young at the age of seven and quite fit and healthy, had suffered a heart attack, and George thought of his mother, Dinah, who had also died of heart fail. The house was cordoned off and disinfected, and all were given gabs to inoculate them from the disease. It was insisted on that Russel's body was cremated. Even in what was considered modern times, you would only go to the hospital if you were actually at death's door and for common ailments such as flu or colds, you wouldn't bother a doctor, you simply took care of these yourself, besides doctors were expensive. Florence lived with the guilt of Russel's death for the rest of her life.

In the year 1937, and their next child came along. "Boy?" said George.

"No, girl," said Florence.

Snow White and the Seven Dwarfs was the movie to see in the cinemas, and George can't help but think to himself, '*That sounds like Florence and the children.*

In the year 1939, the Spanish Civil War ended and Germany invaded Poland by attacking Danzig. Britain's response was to declare war on Germany in defence of Poland.

George Junior, now a teenager, had grown into a big lad, tall and quite stocky. Florence often wondered who he had taken after, it certainly wasn't his father. George Junior was also a bit of a lad in other ways, constantly looking to make a bit of money where ever he could, even if it meant bending the rules a little. George Junior had heard the call from the government asking for all and any unwanted or unused metal to be handed into scape yards to help with the war effort. This metal would be eventually turned into tanks and boats, and thus the scrappy was paying a good price. Over the coming weeks, Norwich City Council began to receive information that the large iron storm drain covers around the Beverly Road, Area, had begun to go missing and this had become a bit dangerous. George Junior knew of a scrappy down Water Works Road that would gladly take and pay for the storm covers despite NCC being written across them. To lift, let alone carry, one of these storm covers was a feat in itself and took a great deal of strength, and it was one of these covers that became the undoing of George. This one cover was jammed, it simple would not budge no matter what George did, it came to be an obsession, and he came up with a cunning plan. George Junior tied a good sturdy rope around one of the stout grills of the storm cover, the other end of the rope held a meat hook, and he sat and he waited. Sure enough, right on time came the number seven bus bound for the city centre and as it stopped to take on passengers, George simple hooked the rope onto the bumper of the bus. The bus pulled away and as the rope uncoiled,

George took the precaution of stepping back from the drain just in case. But he needn't be worried, as the rope went taught, out popped the heavy grill with a ping, George Junior couldn't believe that it had worked, and how clever he'd been with coming up with such a great idea. As George stood revealing in his brilliance, watching the drain clang down the road after the bus, he suddenly realised the bus wasn't going to stop. George ran for a full three streets at full pelt to try and catch the bus, it eventually stopped and George unhooked the rope. All was OK, he had prevented what could have been a bad accident and he had retrieved the drain. The bus pulled away and there on the other side of the road stood the local police constable, arms folded and smiling at George.

In the year of 1940, Italy joined the war on the side of Germany. In Britain, we got a new Prime Minister in the form of Winston Churchill. The evacuation of Dunkirk began and George dearly wished that there was something he could do to help save those poor lads. A restaurant in San Bernardino, California, USA, opened with plans to open up similar restaurants right across the USA, serving the exact same food in each and they called themselves McDonald's, and there was a new addition to the Watkins household in the form of yet another girl.

Just before Christmas of that year, George Senior found George Junior and said, "Go find your brother, Bernard, and I want you to go to Costessey and to that patch of woods I showed you back in the summer, do you remember?" Costessey was then still a village, some five miles northwest of Norwich.

"Yes, I remember," said George Junior.

"Do you remember the Christmas trees in that woods?"

"Yes."

"Good, take this axe and bring us back a nice one for Christmas." Some hours later, the two boys returned, exhausted, sweating and covered in leaf debris and pine needles.

Florence was stood on the front step, baby in arms and shouted for her husband, who shortly came trotting around the corner. "Look, George, look what your boys have brought us." For there lay on the path was a Christmas tree that was all of twenty feet in length and nearly just as round. Christmas morning, and the Watkins were sat in their front room of their house and there sat in the corner was the top two feet of the Christmas tree and piled up alongside the fireplace was a good stack of logs.

The Night the Bombs Dropped

In the year of 1941, HMS Hood was sunk by the Bismarck, and shortly after, the bombing campaign of Great Britain began by the German Air Force and Norwich didn't escape this. During 1942 came what was to be known as the Baedeker raids and Norwich was bombed extensively, particularly during the month of April. Norwich was renowned for its tunnel systems that connected many parts of the city such as the cathedral and the castle to prominent houses. Some of these tunnels went back hundreds of years and most had something to do religious conflict. On the outbreak of war, Norwich City Council had dug an extensive tunnel network under the main central park in the city centre called Chapelfield Gardens. At the sound of the air raid siren, city centre inhabitants were to make their way there for safety. The tunnels were hundreds of metres long and ran across one another at right angles to minimise losses, should there be a direct hit. The tunnels had wireless rooms, infirmary and kitchens, and people would sit on benches that ran the full length down either side. During this time, the tunnel did, in fact, receive a direct hit and many people that particular night did indeed lose their lives.

Because the Watkins family and neighbours were deemed to be just too far outside the city centre to make it to the tunnels in good time, they were given an Anderson Air Raid Shelter to erect in the back garden which annoyed George a little because it took up valuable growing space.

It was evening and the sun was preparing to go down when the first air raid sirens began to wail across the city. George, who had been finishing up in the garden, flung his fork into the soil pronged first while muttering, "Blast." Florence sprang into a carefully prepared plan, and as she gathered up things such as dried food and water, she gave out orders to the children to gather up their bed mattresses and coats, and they did so without question, all the time George protesting the futility of it all. "Do we have to, it will probably all be over in an hour and nothing will have happened just as before."

"George, do as you're told and help me please." Between the two of them, they managed to get everyone down into the Anderson Shelter and settled in good time, and Florence set about entertaining the little ones. There then came the first rumble in the distance which was unnerving as it meant that someone may be on the receiving end of that but the Watkins hadn't in the past experienced much more than this, which was why George was reluctant to go into the shelter in the first place.

There then came the first loud bang and it was close, and the family screamed and drew closer together and a seriousness came over George as he realised that tonight was to be their night on the receiving end. The explosions came faster and closer, they not only heard them but could feel them as the shelter shook and soil fell from the ceiling. Florence could hear her neighbours scream as she pulled the children closer and she begged for it to stop. Then silence, which seemed almost as unnerving as the bombing, was it over, were they to move or stay where they were? This was broken by the sound of a man's voice saying, "Hello there in the shelter, are you OK?" The door opened and there stood the local air raid warden. "Is everyone accounted for?" he asked.

"Yes, we're all here and OK," said Florence.

"Good," he said. "You got a direct hit." Florence launched upwards and out at this news, no it couldn't be, her palace, her home, hit. There came a procession of the whole family heading back down, the garden path towards the house at speed, the warden shouting, "It's not safe," the whole time. But the house was still standing, but as they walked to the front and looked back, they could see a gaping hole in the front roof. Florence dashed through the front door, and up the stairs and into the front bedroom. An incendiary device had come through the roof and had been caught by the bare metal springs of the bed which were now glowing red hot. The device had not detonated properly, if it had the house would now be an inferno, if Florence hadn't asked for the mattresses to be removed, detonated or not, there was a good chance the house would have gone up anyway.

Florence was upset, frightened as she turned to George and said, "See, George, see." These were the only cross words she ever had with George, and George never doubted nor questioned her ever again. They sensibly left the house to let the bomb disposal team do their job. Over this dark period of history in Norwich, many others feared much worst, two thousand homes were entirely destroyed, three hundred and forty people lost their lives and many families were dispersed, and George fought harder than ever to keep his together. That following morning, George biked to work to find Morgan's Brewery had suffered a direct hit, and thankfully, no one was hurt but George was now out of work. This fellow, Hitler, had turned out to be a proper pain in the behind.

In the year of 1943, 617 Squadron of the Royal Air Force flew into the Ruhr Valley, and bombed the Mohne and Eder Dams with the now famous, Barns Wallace, bouncing bombs and brought about the destruction of the industrial heartland of Germany, an act that earned them the name of the 'Dam Busters'. It was also the year that Florence and George had yet another little girl.

The year, 1944, and June 6th, thousands of allied forces stormed the beaches of Normandy, many about the same age as George Junior. The sheer fear those lads must have experienced was incomprehensible, and yet not long after Paris was liberated and Europe was to shortly follow, so began the destruction and annihilation of the Nazis movement.

George went to work in the laundry department of Norwich Hospital, it wasn't physically demanding work, it was more to do with the hours that George had to get used to, but it paid, it put food on the table and kept his family together. In later years, he was able to get his son, Bernard, a job at the hospital too. Bernard had been a gentle child, not soft but mild-mannered and always polite, and he had a great love of animals. Florence remembered fondly an occasion the 'Indian salesman' was doing his usual rounds from door to door selling cleaning products and had spotted him at the end of the street. Florence didn't like to open the door to him, it wasn't racism, Florence didn't know how to be a racist, it had more to do with a lack of knowledge and understanding. "Bernard, that Indian man is about to knock on the door, tell him I'm out, OK?" She then shot up stairs out the way.

Bernard opened the door to a smartly dressed man wearing a turban, he had a silver beard and a moustache that had been waxed at the points, "Good day to you, my good man, is your mother in?"

"No, she's gone out."

"When do you expect her back?"

Bernard turned and shouted up the stairs, "Mum, when are you coming back?"

In the year, 1945, and US Marines raised the Star-Spangled Banner over the Island of Iwo-Jima. The USS Indianapolis was torpedoed with great loss of life, and shortly after, World war Two finally and thankfully came to an end.

In the year of 1946, and George and Florence had a child and guess what, it was a girl, born in January, Gloria Jean was to be their last, and Florence would lovingly refer to her as 'the scrapings of the barrel'.

Over twenty-six years, Florence had fallen pregnant thirteen times and eleven children had survived, two boys and nine girls. Gloria had a good upbringing and fond memories of both her mother and father. Florence was a wonderful mother, loving, humble, she kept a clean house and all the children were dressed well and washed in the morning, and all got a large bowl of porridge before they went to school or work. Florence would make up her husband's sandwiches for work or 'pieces' as she would call them, she would go to jumble sales and buy anything wool more often baby clothes, wash and unpick these and re-knit them into socks for George. George could sometimes be found wearing pink socks. Florence did everything for everybody, she even made sure George had a pouch for his favourite tobacco, 'Digger Flake' whenever needed. She was a loving and caring mother and wife.

George was up early every morning whether working or not. Each night before tea, he would walk up to the Grove Pub for a pint. He was a loving father but firm, he never hit, he never had to. No matter how old the children were, they would all have to be back in the house by ten-thirty every night. He was a great fixer and would repair everyone's shoes and boots better than any cobbler. Each week, he would give Florence eight pounds and she would run the entire house on this, bills, food, everything. On a Sunday, George would work in the garden in the morning, wash up before lunch, and go to the Grove for a couple of pints and a smoke. Gloria would sit and wait for his return as she knew he would have for her a 'threepenny joe', a three pence piece that was gold and in the shape of a fifty pence piece. Gloria would take this up to the corner shop and despite there was still rationing on some things such as sweets after the war, she was still able to buy a bag of sweets that if were any bigger, she would have to throw over her shoulder to carry home. George would sit and eat his Sunday lunch on his own, the children having eaten earlier, and in the afternoon, would have a sleep.

In the year 1947, Pakistan gained independence from Great Britain, Anne Frank's diary was published, and the following year, Mahatma Gandhi was assassinated.

Gloria remembered that there was three to a bed, the boys had a room of their own as did her mother and father. The beds for extra warmth in winter would have army coats thrown over them, one of which was the great coat George had brought from the orphanage. There was a chamber pot under the bed, and in the winter, the inside of the windows would freeze up.

In the year of 1952, Queen Elizabeth II became Queen of England and the Commonwealth. George Junior had been conscripted into the British Army and was subsequently posted to India. George Junior had been away some time when, one Saturday morning, without announcement, in walked George in his army uniform. There was great excitement and greeting, once all had settled down George Junior went to the door and opening it said, "Mother, Father, I'd like you to meet my wife." In walked a young woman, she was Indian and wearing a long brightly coloured sari and shawl, she entered and bowed. She was barefoot and walked to one corner of the room, and sat cross-legged on the floor. Wrapped in the folds of her sari was a tiny baby. Florence and George Senior just stared at each other without word.

George Senior finally got up, folded the newspaper he was reading, tucked it under his arm and on passing his son, said, "Good luck," and went to the pub in his slippers. On his return, George was told that his son, new wife and child were to be

162

staying with them until they found their feet. George Senior knew this all along and had purposely left this to Florence to organise. George Junior's wife spoke not a word of English, she would later become known as Margret and it turned out that the child she was carrying wasn't George's.

"But who are we to judge," said George to Florence. "I seem to recall you and I have been there and done that, my darling." Over the coming years, Florence and Margret became close. Florence taught Margret English, and Margret taught Florence a new style and way of cooking, Margret was an incredibly cook. George Junior gained work on a farm just to the south of Norwich, and some years later, he and Margret moved to Sudbury in Suffolk and one of their three sons, they named Russel, who died tragically as a young man and yet again, this name proved unfortunate for the Watkins family.

In the year 1953, Everest was conquered, and George left the hospital and went to work for Stevenson's Iron Works in Lakenham, Norwich, which he was pleased about. George had always preferred physical work, it kept him fit and healthy. Shortly after he started, George crushed his thumb and had to go to hospital to get it checked. Luckily, it wasn't broken, and the staff bandaged it up and sent George on his way. George stood outside the hospital, it was too late to go back to work, so George sat on a wall, charged his pipe and had a smoke. The thumb that had been damaged and bandaged was the same that he used to pat down the smoking embers of his pipe, and soon, his thumb burst into flames, what followed was a scene straight out of Laurel and Hardy. George jumping around in a panic trying to put out his thumb. Once he had, he walked back into the hospital to be greeted by the same nurse who had bandaged his thumb in the first place, who on seeing what George had done, she rolled her eyes and said, "That smoking will be the death of you, George."

The year of 1956, and the first computer was developed and Elvis went to number one with *Don't Be Cruel*, and *Hound Dog*.

Winter came, and Gloria and local kids were bob sleighing using all they could find, dustbin lids, door mats you name it, when brother, Bernard, came home from work, and on seeing the kids, produced from the boot of his car a long thick rubberised bag that was zipped down the middle. All the kids were able to sit in it one behind the other and hold onto the sides like a toboggan, it worked perfectly. That night at tea, Gloria recounted the story and then asked what her older brother did at the hospital. "Bernard works in the morgue." that night all the kids went to bed smelling of formaldehyde.

In the year 1957, Sputnik was launched into space, and sometime after, Gloria went to work at a local chemical factory called May and Baker, on Sweetbriar Road. Gloria also began to date, and on one occasion, she was stood at the front gate talking to a lad who was to take her out that night. George came up the garden path, grabbed Gloria by the arm and dragging her back into the garden, told the lad to go away. As they entered the house, George said to Gloria, "What have I told you about dating 'Yanks'?"

"What makes you think he was a yank, Father?" said Gloria.

"Because of the sharp suit he was wearing," said George. George was uncomfortable with the amount of English girls that were throwing themselves at Americans just because they had money.

"He's no yank, he's one of the Harrison's from Horning Close," said Gloria.

George, without a word, grabbed his daughter by her arm and marched her around the corner to Horning Close, knocked on the door of the Harrison's and said to the lad, "You are welcome to take my daughter out." Gloria was finding herself, and found she had a passion for hair and hairdressing, having spent long hours preparing her sisters' hair before they went out. Gloria did, at one point, come home, having dyed her hair from black to blond to the indignation of her mother.

Don't Be Cruel

Gloria wanted more, more than just the production line of some factory. She has a God-given gift, a skill, a passion, that of hair. Gloria walked the city and asked at every hairdresser if they needed an apprentice, and finally, she found a shop in Magdalene Street that was prepared to give her a chance, and she secured a deal.

Gloria, with excitement, approached her mother. "Mum, I've got an apprenticeship at a hairdresser in Magdalene Street, I start next week. I'm going to be a hairdresser, Mum."

"And how long will this take?" said Florence.

"Two years, they reckon," said Gloria.

"And how much will it pay, Gloria?"

"Well, once I qualify, I can make as much money as I like."

"No, I mean in the two years of training, Gloria."

Gloria knew where her mother was going with this and hung her head. She wouldn't lie to her mother, and reluctantly, she said, "One pound ten shillings a week, Mum."

"Well, then, the answer no, isn't it?"

"But why, Mum? Why can't I be what I want?" Tears welled up in Gloria's eyes.

"Because, child, you need to give me one pound a week for your keep, seven shillings for your bus fare and you now need to buy your own sanitary towels, so, no, you can't, you're doing all right at the factory, you just concentrate on that and get this silly hairdressing notion out of your head, girl." Florence wasn't being cruel, there was a necessity for the entire family to come first as a whole and Florence couldn't afford for one person to be supported by the rest. It wasn't long after that, however, that Florence was all too pleased for Gloria to leave the factory, for on an afternoon came a mighty explosion at the factory in a room next to where Gloria was working. The explosion was so close and loud but Gloria and others knew nor felt any of the effects and there came great confusion on the appearance of fire engines and panicked people running everywhere. The explosion, however, was heard by the rest of Norwich and a crowd had gathered at the gates of friends and family, and George was one, demanding to know what was happening. A number of hours went by, and finally and thankfully, the work force was allowed to leave and Gloria never went back.

George was stood in the back garden leaning on his fork, puffing on his pipe which he now looked at, for it was the very pipe that Captain Williams had given him on his seventeenth birthday, the very day he had become a man. George now looked off into the distance and thought, *I've come a long way, from a mining village in the Valleys of Glamorgan to the very far-flung corners of this planet to here and my loving family round me, I've done OK for a boy from the valleys.*

Florence had noticed George being thoughtful, she had seen him watching the children and had caught him looking at her in a strange way, something was wrong but George wouldn't say when Florence asked him what was on his mind.

December, 1959, Florence was in the kitchen preparing that evening's meal. It wouldn't be long before her brood would come home hungry and recounting the day's events loudly and all at the same time at the dinner table. Just then, the front door opened. *Who could this be? It's far too early.* she wiped her hands on a tea towel and went to open the kitchen door and was beat by George. "What's wrong, George, why are you home so early from work?"

"I had to pick something up, Florence, are all the children out?"

"Yes, they won't be back for a while."

"Good," said George. Florence had wandered back to her sink when George, holding her shoulders, turned her around and as he did, he went down on one knee. "Florence Christabel Tricker, will you do me the honour of being my wife?"

Florence was completely taken by surprise and said with a chuckle, "What are you doing, you silly man?"

Just then, George pulled a ring box from his pocket and opened it to reveal a diamond engagement ring. "Will you marry me, Florence?"

"Yes, yes, of course, I'll marry you, you gorgeous man. It's only taken you forty years, George, but, at least, you are a man of your word." The two embraced and kissed, and Florence spun in circles of excitement around the kitchen only to stop periodically to say something like, "I need to look at my good dress." Spin, spin. "Invitations." Spin, spin. "Where are we to be married, George?"

"City Hall, Florence." Spin, spin.

Florence stopped and looked at George. "And when's this to be, George?" She was suspecting something.

"This Saturday, Florence."

"What?" shouted Florence, who now flew into a complete panic rushing in and out of doors muttering to herself, "And how are we to get there, George?"

George looked out of the window and said, "The weather's supposed to be fine on Saturday, Florence, I think we'll walk."

The End
Based on a true story.